Sandbar Season

A SUMMER COTTAGE NOVEL

REBECCA REGNIER

Chapter One

Marcia Hope Venerable

Fremont Street in Las Vegas was home to KISS impersonators, showgirls, The Golden Nugget Casino, and vacationers of every stripe ready to try their luck at slots or the blackjack tables.

But this week, it was home to The World's Best Dishes Food Competition as well.

And Marcia Hope Venerable was in the middle of the chaos.

Hope, as her friends called her, had no interest in blackjack tables.

The table she was focusing on was the judges' table.

Incredibly, she was in the finals for the title of World's Best Recipe and for prize money in an amount she didn't even want to consider.

It had been a long road to get here, to be in this spot, and have a chance to win. She still couldn't believe it.

This was her second time in this competition, and she knew one wrong move, and she could easily blow it.

It was a bit weird to be in middle of the entertainment capital of the world, and have no interest in shows or gambling or any of it.

Though maybe she'd go see Donny Osmond once she was eliminated, like the last time she was here. Donny was a childhood crush. That smile! Those purple socks! It would be a good consolation prize to herself.

But she wasn't eliminated.

Hope's dish kept moving through the rounds and up the competition's leader board. Other competitors were falling all around her like so much chocolate souffle, yet she remained.

Maybe, just maybe she could win! But a lot had to go her way before that happened.

Focus. Hope needed to focus if she wanted to keep her dreams alive.

She didn't want to come this far in the competition to, well, only to come this far.

She didn't want to repeat her mistakes from the last time she was here. She'd failed here before, spectacularly.

Two years ago, she'd qualified for The World's Best Dishes Food Competition with her Anna Maria Dream Dessert. It was a family favorite treat for her girls when they went on vacation. She'd entered it into the local qualifying event, and it was a hit with judges too. The sweet, fluffy concoction helped her earn her first trip to Vegas.

She was a rookie food competitor back then. It was a great dish but not a great competition entry. She'd learned those were two separate things.

The dessert required several chilled layers of pudding and creams, and in the heat of Las Vegas, her fluffy dessert had turned into a mushy, soupy mess topped with crushed Oreos.

Yeah, not her best work.

She was as crushed as those Oreos when she'd failed so spectacularly. She thought cooking competitions were her thing, that she'd found her niche, but two years ago it had all gone totally wrong. She could still see the pudding sliding around in the thirteen by nine glass pan. She remembered her ugly attempts to spread Cool Whip over the mess. What an embarrassment!

She only hoped no one saw her disastrous dish. There was no thought of winning, just getting out without anyone noticing her, that was the goal.

This was the one food competition where home cooks and line cooks, and caterers went head-to-head with chefs, bakers, and pit masters. The food was the thing. Not the resume. This was what appealed to her. She didn't have credentials from any culinary institute. But that didn't matter if she made a delicious dish.

A middle aged empty nest mother of two, wife of one, small time caterer, was no match on paper for the chefs in the competition, some of whom ran restaurants in the luxury hotels a few miles away on the strip. Yet here she was, again.

After that defeat the first year, she'd wanted to quit. She felt like an imposter. She wasn't good enough.

But something kept her going. She'd quit on herself so many times before in favor of her husband or her children. That was as it should be, she thought. Putting her dreams ahead of them was selfish.

But now that her children were adults, something had shifted. If she quit; it wasn't selflessness. It was fear. And she feared her husband would never be grown. Using her kids as a reason not to pursue her dreams seemed like a cop out.

Hope told herself that she'd started this to prove something to her girls. They were grown now but she still wanted them to be proud of her. That used to be what she told herself.

But even that wasn't the truth. She wanted to be proud of *herself*. She wanted to prove this to *herself*. Somehow the clock in her life had started ticking faster and faster. It wasn't a wall clock marking hours, but a stopwatch, speeding to some finish line in a race she didn't know she entered.

If she was going to be a woman of substance instead of a woman hanging on by a thread, it was now or never.

Her family thought cooking competitions were Hope's little hobby. It wasn't her hobby. It was more.

So, she failed her first time out, big time, but she didn't quit. She went back home and kept learning. She kept trying new ideas and testing her creations.

And Hope's persistence paid off. In the second year of her local competition, she'd qualified to go to the big show in Las Vegas again with a fantastic hamburger slider. She was so excited; it wasn't a dessert! She could better recreate this dish under pressure and in warm temperatures.

But Archie, her husband, said they couldn't afford to send her to Vegas again.

"Great idea, Hope. How about I just give you this month's mortgage payment so you can go to Vegas again and lose," Archie had said. He sneered when he said it, but even with that annoying sneer, she knew he was right.

This so-called hobby was expensive. Hope had to pay for travel and all her cooking supplies. The World's Best Dishes Food Competition did pay for the hotel, but still, Archie's words rang in her ears. They'd finally crawled out of debt from the girls' college and the Great Recession of the early 2000s. But barely, just barely. There wasn't extra for travel in the Venerable household budget. Though Archie seemed to find money for his pursuits. It was hard not to notice that.

Still, it was selfish for her to go, after how terribly she did the first time.

Year one of The World's Best Dishes Food Competition, Hope had brought a bad recipe to the arena. In year two, she bowed out completely. She watched from home and wondered what might have been.

But this year, this time, Hope took both of her previous failures and used them as fuel to form a new plan.

She perfected a new recipe, developed a creative way to present her dish, and she did it in between earning real money with her catering jobs. She'd parlayed her hobby into a budding career.

During the day, she managed the local Café Maria, a breakfast restaurant in Covington. Covington was in Kentucky just outside of Cincinnati, Ohio. Hope traveled back and forth over the Ohio River border on the weekends to take every catering job she could book. That catering money was her ticket. Archie couldn't say boo about her "extra money."

She'd worked herself ragged. No assistants, no days off. She was surrounded by food day and night. Hope was a woman on a mission. She knew she looked wan and scraggly lately from the effort. But she had a fire in her gut to make this work.

She wouldn't be guilted into staying home this year. If she had a chance to compete in Vegas, she would do it. No regrets.

Hope was fueled by something she had suppressed for decades, something that refused to die, no matter how many times circumstances conspired to kill it.

Hope didn't dare reveal her real dream, even to herself.

She knew there was more to this so-called hobby. A win in Vegas could unlock it.

It took her a year, but she'd squirreled enough away to pay for the trip to Vegas for the competition. This was on top of what she made at the restaurant that paid their normal bills.

But she still had to win her region, Cincinnati, to get to the big competition in Vegas. You couldn't just go to the Las Vegas round, you had to earn it every year.

And she did it! For the third time in a row, she won her region. She proved she was one of the best food competitors in Southern Ohio and Northern Kentucky. Hope qualified for the big show this time with her crustless zucchini pie. She'd kicked the crabcakes out of her competition.

She was on her way again, armed with experience, and answers for Archie or anyone who wanted to tell her it was frivolous or selfish.

If she wanted to prove she was supposed to be here, that she could cook with the best of them,

Hope and her zucchini pie recipe would have to fire on all cylinders.

The competition in Las Vegas included country categories and then the big international finals. It really was the world's best food prepared by the world's best chefs and cooks.

Since she'd won her region in Kentucky and Ohio, Hope earned the right to represent the region for the USA portion of The World's Best Dishes Food Competition.

Several winners would be crowned: appetizers, side dishes, main course, dessert, recipe, and BBQ were this year's categories. The winner in each category got eight thousand dollars and the right to move on to The World's, all being held the same week in Las Vegas.

It was like competing in Miss USA, winning, and then doing it again the next day for Miss Universe, well, without the crowns and swimsuits.

The big winner in The World's Best Dishes Food Competition got one hundred thousand dollars, not a tiara.

Hope was not focused on The World's, at all, really. She was there to do well in the recipe category, that was it. She was there to live down the embarrassment of her first foray two years ago. If she was lucky enough to get an honorable mention on this big stage, with dozens of talented culinary professionals, she'd be over the moon.

Word on the street in the cooking competition community was that the recipe category, her category this time, was the hardest.

She'd learned this from her network of food competition friends. Along with finding a purpose in these food competitions, she'd also found a community.

Just like any community, there was gossip, jealousy, and back-biting. Because there was also money at stake, the competition could be cutthroat.

Hope had learned this was no one's hobby, this was serious business.

But here was also comradery, bonding, and mutual respect.

In the end, she just wanted to make a good showing in the competition. She wanted to do better than her dessert disaster. That was her mark of success. Just get better. Learn.

And then the unthinkable happened.

Marcia H. Venerable, home cook and proprietor of Venerable Catering, won the recipe competition. Her zucchini won!

She'd exceeded her goal. Instead of flaming out, she'd actually leave Vegas with the Best Recipe title and eight thousand dollars!

And that win meant she wasn't done, she was still in it, she'd compete for the biggest food prize you could win.

Marcia Hope Venerable from Covington, Kentucky, was going to go head-to-head in the finals with all the category winners. This was more than she'd ever dreamed. It was almost too much to think about winning The World's Best Dish Title. One hundred thousand dollars prize money? That was more money than she could imagine. That kind of money would be beyond paying bills. It could be life-changing.

Life-changing.

No, best not to think about winning the whole thing. She wasn't going to win the whole thing.

But, if she was there, she'd give it her best. She'd already exceeded her goal when she'd packed her knives to come to Las Vegas, why not go for it all?

Her early failures at cooking competitions had taught her a lot. She had gained valuable experience. It was one thing to cook well, another thing to create your own recipes, and a completely different level of pressure doing that with an audience, under a time crunch, in the middle of the circus that was Las Vegas.

The rules of the competition allowed each competitor to have an assistant or two if they needed it. But Hope didn't have that luxury. She could barely afford her own ticket here, much less fund travel for anyone else. So, while most of the competitors had a sous chef, and it would be nice, Hope was going it alone.

She'd already beat out dozens of competitors from all over the country who'd qualified at a local event like she had. She'd already proven herself in her division. But still, maybe she could win it all!

She dared to dream, but only for a moment. The dream couldn't happen if she lost focus on reality. The reality was that she needed to give her best energy to this dish if she stood a chance. She needed to keep a cool head if she didn't want to flame out and embarrass herself in front of culinary luminaries.

She believed in creating food with a good heart and sweet intentions. She had cooked in a sour mood before, and it always led to failure. Hope believed that a good heart led to good food, she believed it to her core.

No matter how often Archie laughed at that and told her it was ridiculous, she cooked with joy.

She called it her Happy Kitchen philosophy.

"The greatest chefs in the world swear and smoke and think they're better than everyone else. Your happy kitchen idea is juvenile, so you'll never get anywhere," Archie said. And then, of course, he ate the entire meatloaf she'd made for him.

Hope had to push away the doubters and her own insecurities.

She'd made it this far. She was one of a handful of competitors vying for The World's Best Dishes Food Competition prize money and bragging rights.

On the day of the finals, she approached the competition with peace, gratitude, and joy to be at this place in her life.

A giant swath of space on Fremont Street was cordoned off. Competitors cooking stations were side by side, three rows deep. Spectators could file by and watch the competitors do their thing. A lot of the competitors had their own personal cheering section.

Of course, Archie wasn't there, neither were her daughters. Julia had her job in New York, and Sara, well, who knew what was up with her?

She decided that was okay, she didn't have to worry about anything but the competition. All the better for her to focus.

And no matter what, Hope was going to enjoy how far she'd come in her food journey.

Chapter Two

Hope

The day of the main competition had arrived. And Hope was ready.

She'd practiced over and over. One thing she knew from her cooking competition experiences was that something different went wrong every time. Nothing went according to plan, ever.

Winners adapted. They modified. They handled problems with ovens, or desert heat changing the temperature of the ingredients, or the portable refrigerators that, no matter what the setting, nearly froze things that were supposed to just be chilled.

It was all fair game. You had to pivot and adjust constantly.

Competitors had one hour to create their dishes and present them to the judges' table.

The first few minutes of the hour went well. Hope turned on her oven to preheat and began to lay out her ingredients.

She would follow the steps she'd practiced over and over. Her recipe was more than ingredients and temperatures and presentation. Each dish she prepared was a choreographed dance. Hope moved through her cooking space with ease. And she gained energy from the spectators watching her do her thing.

But something told her to interrupt her normal steps, to check the oven early on. Sixth sense? Experience? Maybe even a healthy smidge of paranoia.

The oven wasn't right. It wasn't getting hot enough, fast enough. Marcia used her own thermometer to check. While the oven temperature dial read three-fifty, her thermometer told her differently. The oven was barely three-twenty. A less experienced competitor would assume because the dial said three-fifty, the oven was three-fifty. But it wasn't. The oven was running cool.

So, Hope adapted. There was no way to get a new oven and no sense in wasting time complaining to the contest referees. She nudged the dial higher, and she moved faster. Hope had aimed to take her time getting her ingredients perfectly prepared, but instead, she picked up her pace.

She'd need to get her crustless pie in earlier because it would take longer to cook; she'd also need to compensate for the longer bake. This could mean the dish could wind up too dry, so she upped the liquid ingredients. Competitors couldn't add an ingredient that wasn't on their preapproved list, but they could change quantities based on taste, temperature, and whatever conditions presented themselves.

Adapt, adjust, test, pivot, and above all, keep your cool in the Vegas heat. Hope did it all. Instead of swearing or panicking, she remembered her Happy Kitchen philosophy and tried to stay in that zone, even under this scrutiny.

Her local judges called this Crustless Zucchini dish "better than crack." A recipe that was "better than crack" didn't just happen. You made it happen with every shake of salt and stir of the spatula.

Hope felt ease and happiness with how it all turned out, even before she put her dish in the oven. She had been in cooking competitions where she couldn't find a flow. Where it was stop and start. Where no matter what she did, incessant hiccups interrupted the process. But not this time. She moved fluidly, handled problems, and rode her nerves to her benefit instead of letting them spin her heart rate out of control.

She stayed on target.

Competitors had a ten-minute window to present plated food to the judges' tent. That was it. Other times, Hope had been in the position of having to run to the judges' table, pushing a cart, or balancing a tray, with only a second to spare. But not this time. She took her dish out of the oven. She plated the required number of servings in her adorable crème-colored ramekins. She took care to make sure each serving looked perfect, with a meticulously placed medallion of zucchini perched on the rim.

She had a dozen to get just right. She didn't want to risk one rogue judge getting an ugly serving and then marking her entry down for presentation or inconsistency.

Hope looked over her dishes one last time, and with a full three minutes to spare, she placed them on the tray.

She took a deep breath and settled the tray in her arms.

She had a sea of spectators to weave through without dumping the tray all over.

The lane from the kitchen set-ups to the judges' tent was now like the *Fast and the Furious*. If you got in the way, you'd be so much roadkill.

On the first day of competition, two cooks in the burger category crashed into each other and sent their dishes flying. They were both knocked out of the running.

Hope wasn't going to trip on the way to the finish line. She sailed forward, past other competitors who were in the throes of abject panic.

This was it. If you hadn't finished plating by now, your dish might taste great, but the odds were you didn't have time to take the care required to make it look lovely.

Originality and, of course, taste were important, but if you slapped something down that looked sloppy, you'd lose valuable points.

Her crustless zucchini pie dish looked lovely; she knew that she hadn't left it to chance. She glided past the spectators. She didn't hear the clapping.

This was food as sport, no doubt. And part of the sport was being fueled, not flummoxed, by the crowd.

Hope kept her focus. She got to the window and carefully submitted her entry. They checked her badge: Marcia H. Venerable, Recipe Competitor.

She signed a card, verifying that she was turning in her entry. She watched as they took it away, into the tent, to the twelve judges who would taste all the entrees and decide which was the very best and which cook would win the title and one hundred thousand dollars.

She felt calm, satisfied, and accomplished. It had taken her more than an hour to get this dish to the judges. It had taken her a lifetime, really.

And there was nothing to be done now but wait.

Chapter Three

Libby

"You've reached Venerable Catering. Please leave a message, and I'll get right back to you."

Libby left a message. It was weird, she knew, and Hope was going to feel like the past came out of nowhere. "Hi, I haven't seen you in thirty years, and you need to get to Irish Hills immediately." No. That was not going to work. She needed Hope to come to Irish Hills, and she needed to figure out how to make it seem like a logical thing to do.

Hope, they knew her as Hope. In their Sandbar Sister days, she hated the name Marcia, so she went by her middle name, Hope. Hope Benton had become Marcia H. Venerable. Libby wouldn't have had a clue to search that name on Facebook or the internet. Somehow her aunt had it all figured out.

She found the article on Hope's recipe win in Cincinnati and that she would be competing in Vegas.

"Go to that competition, make sure she can do what we need, and then make her an offer she can't refuse."

"Aunt Emma, I'm not Don Corleone."

"Well, you're a high-powered gal. You know how to close a deal. Is it better in person or email with these things?" Aunt Emma had pointed to Libby's smartphone.

"That's an easy answer. In-person always wins. Much harder to look someone in the eye and turn them down."

"And from what you've explained, to get the grant money for this downtown Irish Hills renovation, you need a detailed description about what goes in each building. Seems to me the restaurant is the lynchpin."

"You do understand."

Libby had been lured back to Irish Hills and had decided to stay due to no small amount of scheming from her aunt. And more than that, she'd agreed to fight for the town against corporate developers.

Somehow, she'd become the leader of the Save Irish Hills Community Development Corporation. It had all happened so fast.

But it was right. Libby knew it. As sure as she knew she looked terrible in small floral prints.

They had an uphill fight, but that was okay. A little incline toned your thighs anyway.

Libby had a stretch of buildings to renovate and fill. There was no doubt that Irish Hills needed a restaurant.

The proposal she'd sent the Small Business Downtown Revitalization Authority included renderings that imagined a restaurant downtown. They had the renderings but not the restaurant.

Hope Benton, aka Marcia H. Venerable, could be the perfect person to take this on.

But Libby hadn't been able to get a hold of her. This wasn't something they had months to pull off. It was more like weeks.

They needed this place open soon.

Aunt Emma had pawned an antique necklace, an heirloom, for repairs to the strip of vacant buildings in downtown Irish Hills.

She'd spent her actual savings to block out-of-town developers from getting their hands on the town and turning it into a rest stop.

Libby herself pawned her wedding ring to fund the plumbing and electrical work.

They'd done it because Libby was sure they could secure a grant from the Small Business Downtown Revitalization Authority. That was five hundred thousand dollars. That would be enough to make downtown attractive for everything from restaurants to boutiques.

Well, that was the plan, anyway. Unfortunately, another town was in the running. Covert Pier on Lake Michigan also wanted that money for downtown revitalization. And they were farther along. They had more than plans. They had a restaurant already started. They had Lake Michigan.

Irish Hills needed a restaurant opened downtown, now, yesterday really. Aunt Emma said Hope was the person to do it. Aunt Emma's plan was better than Libby's, since Libby didn't have a specific plan for a restauranteur. She'd barely had the time and money to get the roof on, and now she needed a full-fledged business up and running under it.

So Libby's current mission was to convince her old friend to come back to Irish Hills and open an eatery. It was madness, really, that Libby had returned. She thought the odds of convincing Hope to do the same were low.

Aunt Emma wasn't worried. And she wasn't above using good old-fashioned bribery or blackmail to get her way.

Extortion wasn't Libby's style, but a little bribery? Maybe. Aunt Emma had transferred a lot of vacant lakefront property to Libby, maybe she could use that for the bribery component.

"And don't forget to tell her, no rent on the building and no rent on the cottage."

Aunt Emma had spent her life savings and sizable inheritance to buy land and homes in her own effort to stave off corporate development. Between the two women, they owned property all over the area. Now it was up to Libby to figure out how to stave off total bankruptcy for her aunt and herself. A lot was riding on Libby's ability to rehab an entire town. *A lot.*

"The one on Orchard Beach and Cottage?" Libby ran through the catalog of stuff they had between the two of them to rent, sell, or renovate. The cottage on Orchard Beach was tiny, but it was right on the lake, and it was adorable. It didn't have heat and only one bathroom, but you couldn't beat the view.

"Yes, talk about a stroll down memory lane."

"Right, her grandparents' old farm stand was on Manitou Road, on the other end. She'll drive right by the old place to get to Orchard Beach if she says yes. Nothing like pulling at the heart-strings."

Libby remembered the fresh corn on the cob, the juicy peaches, and the giant tomatoes at the old Benton Farm Stand. Hope did, too. She had to.

"Well, her kids are grown, and her husband is puny; in my opinion, the cottage is plenty of room for now."

"Aunt Emma, you shouldn't be creeping on social media."

"Pshaw. Go to Vegas. If you can't convince Hope to come home to Irish Hills, lure some other chef. They're going to be crawling all over with that contest underway. It's like the Super Bowl of cooking."

"Where did you hear that?"

"I saw that on TikTok."

"You're pretty with it for ninety-something."

"You should see me dance! I've almost got the moves to Lizzo's new song down perfectly!"

Libby was amazed by her eccentric aunt, but in the end, the woman was committed to the plan fully. Libby was, too, so it was time to nicely bribe her old friend to join the cause.

Libby flew from Detroit to McCarron Airport, took an Uber

to Fremont Street, and watched, in awe, as her old friend, a charter member of the Sandbar Sisters, cooked her heart out.

The odds were stacked against this plan. Libby's life had been in total disarray when she'd taken a detour back to Irish Hills. But Hope seemed to be thriving. She'd won the recipe contest the day before and was now one of ten competing to be the best cook in the world!

It was amazing. Hope's life had turned out beautifully, and she was at the top of her game in a competitive field. Libby was so proud of who Hope had become.

Still, maybe there was a chance that Hope felt the same about Irish Hills as Libby did.

And as her aunt had pointed out, if Hope said no, this place was teeming with amazing cooks. Maybe someone here would jump at the opportunity Libby was offering.

Libby watched as Hope glided through her food preparation. She seemed to glow with purpose as she added ingredients, mixed them in her bowl, wielded her little thermometer, and sampled her work along the way before moving to the next step.

Libby watched as her friend lent a competitor a stick of butter in the adjacent kitchen station. She did it with a wink and a smile. Hope was generous where Libby would have been throwing elbows and trying to win.

Hope was in competition with these people, but she was being gracious.

In the woman, Libby could see the girl she'd rode bikes with, got sunburned with, and who was an integral part of their little summer gang of girls.

Her chestnut hair was mostly white in the front. A huge lock of it grabbed your attention when you looked at her. Right now, Hope's thick hair was pulled up and away from her face. Still, the snowy white locks glowed from her widow's peak. Libby was envious. She had gray, not white, and nothing glowy about it. Libby needed J.J. and a day in the salon to keep her hair color. Hope was rocking the white streaks like, well, a rock star.

Her face had changed in thirty years. A few crinkled lines at the eyes, and a furrow at the brow, marked the decades. They were signs of whatever Hope had endured during her life. Good and bad. No matter how life had unfolded, by the time you got to fifty, well, everyone who got this far had lived through something. Ups and downs.

But it was the same Hope: the warmth, the little flirt in the smile she gave to her fellow competitors, her deep laugh as a spectator cheered how she garnished her dish. Libby would recognize that laugh anywhere, anytime.

And Hope's eyes hadn't changed. Libby remembered Hope's eyes. They were the color of amber; they had sealed the doom of the hearts of teen boys throughout the county back in their day.

Libby watched as the competitors turned their dishes in.

In an hour, they'd all find out how they fared.

It was so exciting.

Libby decided to wait. This was an important moment for Hope. After the announcement, she'd look for an opportunity to approach Hope with her offer.

The offer she couldn't refuse if Aunt Emma had it right.

Hope

The cooking competition world was small.

Hope had a lot of friends who'd made it to the finals in other categories. She clapped for Carmel Turro, a friend she'd met when they placed one and two in a cream cheese baking competition a few years back. Carmel won the dessert category here in Vegas. Hope was so excited for her!

When they announced Ally Kid's name as the finalist for the best sandwich, Hope hooted and hollered. Ally had been her roommate when they both auditioned for a cooking reality show. Neither made it far on *The Devil's Diner*, but they had supported each other as they withstood taunts from celebrity Chef Rami Ellston, the program's host.

"You call this risotto? I call it risot-no!"

It was all part of the show, but it stung when Chef Ellston called them hacks. He was there now in Vegas. He was signing cookbooks, visiting the competitors as they worked, and he couldn't have been nicer. He was on stage now, announcing winners. He was smiling and supportive.

Still, Ally and Hope had not enjoyed being screamed at by Chef Ellston for the TV auditions. It had soured Hope from auditioning for other programs like it. Ally kept at it and even won the prize on an episode of *Chop or Flop*. Hope had decided TV wasn't her dream. Food, not TV, was her happy place.

Hope cheered when Sandy Lamb got an honorable mention in the special Chili cookoff event. Chili wasn't a category in the competition, but every year they had a special event, and this year it was Chili. Sandy had won the very first recipe contest in Vegas a decade ago. She was a legend and still knocking it out of the park. She was also generous with tips and tricks to keep your cool in this unique environment.

Hope high-fived her friend Beth Plummer as Beth took to the stage to collect her honorable mention in the burger entrée category.

And everyone in the crowd cheered for Poppa BBQ. The pitmaster couldn't lose. He was unstoppable, and pitmasters all over the country wanted to unseat him. Poppa BBQ had beat her out in a chicken wing contest a few years ago. Getting bested by Poppa BBQ was an experience many of her fellow food sport competitors shared. Poppa BBQ used this year's event to announce that next year he wouldn't be competing. He would be judging. That sent a murmur of excitement through the crowd. Maybe next year, someone else might take the crown without Poppa BBQ in the mix.

It was cutthroat in the competitive food world, but there was support and comradery. Hope had learned so much. And she was genuinely happy for every winner. Everyone there understood the work, the stress, and the disappointments on the road to winning.

Hope waited for the winners' announcement with a grateful heart as she thought of her cooking friends. What a journey this had been. She'd forged a path in this part of her life without the girls or Archie. Maybe she shouldn't be sad about that but proud. She was part of a little food family full of diverse and talented cooks.

And then it was time. Hope stood among hundreds of spectators as Celebrity Chef Rami Ellston took center stage with a microphone in hand. He dramatically announced that was time to reveal the final results to the crowd on Fremont Street.

This was it! The competitors in The World's Best Dishes Food Competition had done their best. Hope had done her best. She held her breath.

Chef Ellston announced third place.

Second place.

A little wave of heartbreak bit at Hope's chest. She didn't think she'd win, but now she saw it hadn't gone as well as she'd thought. She had hoped to place. Still, it had been an amazing few days. Hope was in the midst of managing her attitude and almost missed the winner announcement.

"The winner of The World's Best Dishes Food Competition is Marcia H. Venerable and her Crustless Zucchini Pie!"

Hope heard a scream.

Carmel was cheering for her. Her? Had they just said her name?

Was she the winner?

"Come on up here, Marcia H. Venerable!" Chef Ellston gestured her toward the stage as though they were old friends.

Hope nodded. She put one Croc in front of the other but was really floating on air. Somehow, she was on stage; Chef Ellston smiled with his whiter-than-white teeth and handed her a giant check.

Hope looked out to see Poppa BBQ cheering for her. Beth, Sandy, Ally, and all of her food competitor friends were clapping. It was surreal. She'd won the whole thing!

She smiled for the camera and posed with the check. Chef Ellston was beaming, and also genuinely gracious. He helped her navigate pictures and the weirdness of being on the Fremont Street stage with a giant check in her hand.

"Good show, luv, come a long way from that tragic risotto," Chef Ellston said. She laughed. He did know who she was.

"Thank you, Chef."

"Call me Rami. You earned it. Bang-up job. Maybe we can have you back on *The Devil's Diner* as a judge."

Hope nodded as though that was a thing she could do. Yeah, sure, a judge on *Devil's Diner*. Was she dreaming?

Soon Hope was surrounded by her foodie friends. There were more pictures and congratulations. She answered questions for a popular foodie website, the local paper in Las Vegas, and the Best Dishes PR Team.

This was a trip, a dream, one of the strangest moments of her life, to say the least.

Finally, it died down, with promises to meet up at the reception in the ballroom of their hotel. She had Chef Ellston's card, a card from some agent, and a giant ceremonial check to figure out how to get back to her room.

Hope packed up her equipment and plopped the giant show check on her wheeled cooler. While other revelers in Vegas drank, danced, and gambled, Hope made her way back down Fremont Street to The Golden Nugget, where she was staying.

Is this how Super Bowl players or tennis stars feel after they win? Strangely pedestrian, like you still have to schlep your gear back to your room? She imagined Serena Williams walking down the street with her Wimbledon trophy under one arm and her purse in the other.

It made her laugh to herself. She had just achieved a pinnacle, but she still had to wheel her stuff back. Alas, it wasn't really Queen for Day. It was more Queen for an Hour. Still, not too shabby, even for a short time.

Hope finally managed to lug her stuff back and wheel it all into her room. She took a few deep breaths.

Wow, she'd won. The big check was for show, but the real prize money was being directed deposited to her. One hundred thousand dollars. The thought of that made her lightheaded.

Hope needed a shower before the reception. She probably smelled like cigarettes and parmesan cheese. She also knew she couldn't stay out late.

Her flight was early in the day tomorrow; there was no room in her budget for an extra few days to relax. Well, that wasn't strictly true. She *could* stay another day. But splurging with her prize money wasn't in her nature. The money wasn't the end of the road. It was a beginning. She wasn't sure to what, but she figured it was a nest egg or a seed or some other metaphor. The money was the freedom to choose what came next.

On that note, she figured if she was going to have fun with her foodie friends at the reception, she best be all set for departure tomorrow.

Hope picked up her phone. The battery charge was low. Before she left for the reception, she wanted to text her kids and Archie to tell them the news.

Hope plugged in her phone to charge it and decided to use the iPad instead. She hadn't used it much, but she'd brought it as a backup on the trip. If nothing else, maybe she'd load a movie for the flight home.

She opened the iPad and saw there were a dozen messages.

Maybe more congratulations on the big win!

She opened the messages app on the iPad.

Her mouth dropped open. She blinked her eyes to try to adjust to what she was seeing.

First up, a naked woman. Had she been hacked? Was this spam? Was she about to crash her device?

Hope swiped through the messages. Naked up top, naked down below, naked, naked, naked.

What the heck?

And then she recognized a naked man.

Oh no. Oh my goodness!

That was a familiar, uh, no. It couldn't be.

Hope scrolled down. She recognized the duvet cover, the light gray striped one she'd gotten on sale at T.J. Maxx. This wasn't just her husband with some naked woman; it was her bedroom!

And then, there were a few texts to drive home the awful truth.

"You were so hot last night, so glad we have one more day."

"When does she get home?"

"Sunday afternoon. Driving herself from the airport. So, we have until lunch at least."

Archie and this "hot" naked woman were having a grand old time in Hope's bed on her duvet cover. She loved that duvet cover.

Wait, was it the new receptionist they'd just hired at the dealership? Hope didn't really care who it was. Her husband, the father of her children, the man she'd delayed her own dreams to support, was having an affair.

She was in a whirlwind of anger, betrayal, and disbelief when a knock at the door interrupted this discovery that Archie was cheating on her.

Chapter Five

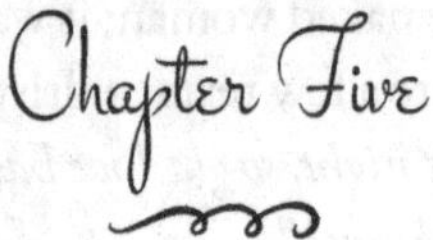

Hope

A knock at the door sounded like it was coming from another planet. Hope moved toward the muted sound, the louder sound, the one she couldn't shake, was the sound of her own ears ringing. The images she'd just seen were still in her vision, not the door in front of her.

Maybe she was going to pass out? Or throw up?

Hope gripped the iPad with one hand and opened the hotel room door with the other.

A stranger was standing there, she had her hand out for a handshake.

"Hope, do you remember me? I'm Libby Quinn, I—"

The tall, beautiful redhead may as well have been speaking another language. Hope didn't process the words coming out of the woman's mouth. The images she'd just viewed, what they meant, how she'd been lied to, made a fool of all, dominated her senses.

"Hold this, will you." She flipped on the camera for the iPad and placed it in the red-headed woman's hands.

"Can you just snap a picture of me, really quick? A little selfie."

"Of course, sure." The redhead held up the iPad and pointed it toward Hope.

Hope grabbed her giant check and positioned herself for the camera.

Hope smiled—or thought she did. Maybe it actually looked like she was baring her teeth? No matter. If her face was ambiguous, her hand gesture wasn't.

With one hand, she flipped the bird. With the other, she held up the giant check. The red-headed stranger in her room cocked her chin to the side but didn't question the gesture.

"Thanks." Hope took the iPad back and hit send. The next thing Archie and his naked friend would see would be Hope and a bunch of money. "Take that, Archie."

The woman at the door inched in a bit more.

Hope tried to get her heart to find a normal rhythm. She took a deep breath and then another. "I'm sorry, you said your name. Are you from the competition? I still need to change before the reception."

Hope really looked at the woman now. There was something familiar.

"I'm not, Hope. It's me—"

And Hope said the woman's name with her.

"Libby!"

"Yes."

"What are you doing here?"

"I've come at a bad time."

"I'm having the weirdest day."

"Congratulations, by the way, that win was so awesome."

"Yeah, yeah, but then, I came here to find *this*! This is my husband's hairy back, and this is the woman who works at his office, I think. New receptionist. Nice, huh?" Hope didn't normally share her life story with strangers. But technically, this wasn't a stranger, and her life story didn't normally take this kind of turn.

"Oh, Hope, I'm so sorry! That's terrible."

Hope hadn't seen this woman for decades, but somehow, she felt so unhinged that she was spilling details of the intimate disaster that was her marriage.

"I mean, Archie and I had problems. From the get-go, we had problems, but we were a team. We were working to pay off the house, we were almost there, and to sell it, and to maybe someday I could—"

She stopped herself. This was a stranger. It had been decades. She and Libby had exchanged their deepest secrets, hopes, dreams, and Forenza Sweaters, but that was long before they were adults. This pulled-together woman didn't look like she would understand a thing about Hope's dreams these days or disappointments.

"Look, I'm here at the exact right time. Not the wrong time."

"Yeah, me unraveling in my hotel room in Vegas." Hope sat down on the bed; she felt her spine slump over. The joy, the sense of accomplishment she'd just felt, were crushed, pulverized by the hammer of her actual life.

"I am here with an offer, something I think you'd be perfect for."

"What?" Hope had no idea what Libby did for a living, where she lived, or what kind of offer she'd be in a position to make.

"I was very recently in a similar situation to you."

"Oh yeah, your husband too dumb to know what a shared iCloud is?"

"Ha, no, too addicted to gambling to see that siphoning money from the non-profit I founded could land him and me in prison."

That stopped Hope in her self-pitying tracks. Of course, she didn't know Libby's troubles or anything about her life. It was hard to see someone else when your vision was clouded with your own unfolding drama. She felt like a heel.

"Oh, Libby, I'm so sorry. You married Henry Malcolm, right? That was the last I heard from my mom." Hope remembered how she heard it too. Her mother had hung it out as an example of someone doing things "the right way" versus how Hope and Archie had been forced to marry quickly before the first semester was even underway in her freshman year of college.

Ugh. What a mess that was, second only to the current one.

"I did, and it was okay for a decade or two...until it wasn't. Anyway, I moved back to Irish Hills. I'm working to revitalize the town."

"Wow, I miss the lake. I never got back after that summer in 1989." An image of her grandpa's farm stand, and her grandmother's little kitchen, flashed in her mind. The smell of her beach towel drying on the line. It all came back in a rush. Hope wondered if the central nervous system was supposed to know how to process all this information from different points of her life careening around her brain at the same time.

She was feeling decidedly nauseous. So maybe the answer to that question was no.

"Same, but let me tell you, returning to Irish Hills was just what I needed. Oh, and J.J. is still in town."

J.J. Libby, Goldie, and Viv, her Sandbar Sisters. She had thought of them often, wondered, when she had a moment, where life had taken them.

A swirling dark cloud separated her youth in Irish Hills from her adulthood. She then blurted out a fact she barely let herself unpack. Her life didn't have room for it.

"Well, I mean, we did maybe nearly kill a guy. I have great memories, but then, the tornado." That day nearly destroyed Irish Hills. They'd protected themselves from the elements for sure and protected J.J. from her mother's abusive boyfriend. When she framed it that way, it was okay. She could live with herself. But if she really looked at it, did they contribute to a man being swept away in the storm because they wouldn't let him into the cellar at Nora House?

Libby took Hope's hands in hers. She smiled softly. She was one of five women on the planet that this likely haunted in the same way.

"Oh, we didn't kill anyone. It's a long story. But we didn't. That guy, Bruce? Yeah, Aunt Emma basically drove him out of town. Not us. Not the tornado. But I get it. I stayed away, in part, because of that."

Hope returned the smile, and then it felt like her legs might not support her much longer. She needed to sit down. She needed to let her body catch up to all the input her brain was getting. The cooking victory, the marriage failure, and now the relief that they actually didn't hurt anyone back in their teen years. It was a lot.

Libby seemed to understand and guided her to the chair in the corner of her hotel room.

"I'm going to get you a glass of water," Libby said.

"Yes, okay, thank you."

Libby busied herself with that, and Hope tried to unspool all the threads knotting her up.

Hope didn't often take out memories and turn them over, examine them, or try to understand how they brought her to where she was. She didn't have time for that. It didn't serve her to look back.

In a few short minutes, Hope felt like she'd taken a high-speed tour of her life, from summers at the lake to the horror in Vegas. And she'd wound up asking a near stranger to send a picture of her making obscene gestures in response to obscene pictures.

Libby handed her a glass of water. Hope noticed Libby's tasteful manicure. She wore a delicate gold bracelet on her wrist. Her strawberry blonde highlighted hair of their youth had deepened to a rich auburn color. Her clothes were casual—jeans, a navy blue blazer, and a simple white blouse—but they were expensive and well made.

Libby was the rich girl in their group. She'd come from money. Who was Libby Quinn now?

Well, right now, she was there, offering an ear and a glass of water. That was how it was going to have to go, one minute at a time, until Hope found some equilibrium.

"Okay, well, great, we didn't kill a guy. One less thing to feel crappy about. Good deal." Hope realized she was sounding flippant over a serious issue. "I'm sorry, I have just so much to process right now. And I have to be at this reception, and I smell like fried zucchini and heartache."

"Nothing to be sorry about, truly. But, well, I am about to throw another thing your way. I promise it's a good thing."

"Why not? It's been that kind of day." Hope was really only half-listening. Numb. She'd moved from dizzy to numb. Was numb better?

"So, my offer. I have the perfect space for you to open a restaurant in the new and improved Irish Hills, also a charming lakeside cottage to stay in while you do it."

"Excuse me?" It felt like Libby was speaking a different language. Open a restaurant? Lakeside cottage?

Libby pressed on. "You are the best cook on the entire planet. I just witnessed that. You'd be the jewel of downtown Irish Hills. I think people would come for miles to eat at your place."

"So, you know I cook. I cater and manage a restaurant—but open my *own* restaurant? I haven't ever done that. I'm not experienced. I don't want this win to give you the wrong idea."

"Yes, haven't you ever dreamed of opening your own restaurant? Based on what I just saw you do out there, you have to have."

Hope had dreamed that. More than once. More times than she could count.

"I do. I used to. It's a lot harder than people make it seem. Financially, physically, and managing it, and marketing. It's just a lot." Hope knew the realities of running a restaurant. She'd played them out in her head. Over and over.

"I know, but you're up to it. I can see you are. You know how great it is in Irish Hills. don't you miss the lake? How we all grew up together there?"

Libby was selling her now. Hope could feel that and was wary about buying into it. She was vulnerable. Her life was in total chaos in this moment.

"I haven't had the luxury of that, of looking back." In truth, Hope didn't want to look back because there was regret. There were dreams she'd deferred until they died. Or almost died.

"It's been a revelation for me too, being back there, where we all had the best times."

"Look, Libby, you've always been well off. And by the looks of things, you still are. I don't have that kind of bank account." Hope didn't want to be mean, but the woman in front of her was to the manor born. That was what Hope's mother called it. Hope didn't hold it against Libby but dabbling in opening a restaurant was no big deal if money wasn't a concern.

"I'm saying, you don't have to have the bank account. I've got the space. A gorgeous space, really. And it's rent-free, as long as you need it to be. Zero for the lease, and it's nearly ready to have a chef like yourself come in and make the final tweaks. Plus, I have this cottage sitting empty, right on the water on Orchard Beach. You can stay there, no rent. It's empty."

"You have an empty restaurant and an empty cottage?"

"Well, Aunt Emma owns the buildings downtown. She dumped—I mean, gifted me, a lot of property, but honestly, you don't know the half of it. I have an empty dance pavilion too."

It was now Libby who looked a little unsettled, recounting whatever was going on in Irish Hills.

Hope remembered the dance pavilion, roller skating dates at night, and days filled with cocoa butter and lemonade.

"Libby, you're sort of talking crazy. And I'm in no spot to make major life changes."

"Honey, you're in the perfect spot. Listen, we let the Sandbar Sisters float away. That's the real shame of our past. Or maybe thinking we'd make friends like that everywhere we went. You don't. Well, I didn't."

Hope realized she hadn't either, not really. Libby continued to make her case.

"I know we're better together. And if you've ever dreamed of opening a restaurant, it can happen. I can help you make it happen. I'm good at getting things like that going. It's my specialty, community development. This community in Irish Hills needs you. I need you!"

It all sounded so sweet, perfect. But it was a dream. Hope's reality was bare ass naked on the iPad. And it was the farthest thing from sweet.

"Thank you, Libby, but I have to say no. I have a mess to clean up with Archie. It's not the right time."

"I'd say it's the perfect time. You have a big fat check and a clear indication of who not to spend it on," Libby said and nodded toward the iPad and Archie.

"Again, I have to pass, but you know. Come with me to the reception. I have an extra ticket, and no family came with me. We can have a drink or two. And you can tell me about your life, Henry, kids? All of it."

"How about I tell you that I just kissed Keith Brady? The last time I did that, I think Wham was at the top of the charts."

"Oh my gosh! He's still there?"

"Still there, and still a super fox."

Hope laughed, and another face from the past flashed in front of her eyes. "Wow, good for you. Give me twenty minutes. We'll go over to the reception together if you have the time. It's at the Stirling Grand. We can have a glass of wine, catch up?"

"Stirling Grand, ugh, but sure, that's perfect."

"Why the ugh?"

"Oh, nothing, just let's focus on you."

"Awesome, I can drown my sorrows and celebrate, depending on how the wind blows."

Hope's answer to Libby's fanciful offer was decidedly no. But that didn't mean the two of them couldn't enjoy a few hours together.

In a few hours, Hope would have to get on a plane home and deal with the Archie Situation. A glass of wine with an old friend before the dreaded confrontation might be the best thing for her.

And maybe this Archie Situation was a two or three glass of wine situation or three or four shots.

Chapter Six

Hope, 1989

Hope squished her beach chair down in the sand and angled herself toward the sun. The sky was pure blue. They'd taken the pontoon boat out to the sandbar. Hope looked up through one squinted eye.

Any cloud that had tried to form was quickly incinerated by the sun.

"Am I good?" she asked Goldie, who was squirting her already blond hair with a yellow spray bottle of Sun In.

Goldie assessed Hope's positioning.

"Yep, no shadows."

God forbid there'd be a shadow anywhere on her entire body. What a waste of baby oil that would be!

Hope had learned her lesson about Sun In two summers ago. Sun In turned blonde hair blonder, dishwater blonde hair vibrant. But it had turned Hope's brown hair orange. Her grandpa said he'd never seen that color in nature before. Luckily, grandma didn't give a care as long as she got rid of it before her mother saw it.

While Libby, J.J., Viv and Goldie had almost zero supervision during the summer, Hope had to deal with periodic marshal law. Her grandparents owned the little farmhouse in Irish Hills. They let her stay all summer and work at the farmstand, which she loved. Her grandparents were okay with her coming and going as long as she did her chores.

But every few weekends, her parents would show up, and it was constant questions.

"Where are you going? When will you be back? How many people are going to be there? Are the parents home?"

Ugh. Constant.

Libby's Aunt Emma stepped in and assured Hope's mother that she was always present at Nora House. Hope's mother said Libby and Emma were "Old Money." She said it with a reverence that was grody. But, because Aunt Emma seemed fancy to Hope's mom, that worked to loosen Hope's leash a bit when they were in Irish Hills. If she said she was going to Libby's, or hanging out on the sandbar with Libby, or at Nora House, her mom shut up.

Most of the time, that was true, but Hope also sneaked to summer concerts and dates under the banner of going to Libby's. Libby was good cover.

Genius really. And it was the only way to deal with her mom's annoying questions.

Hope's mom was her obstacle. Hope had plans, a lot of them, and her mom was one hundred percent against anything Hope wanted to do.

But lying in the sun with her friends was the perfect time to share what she really wanted in life. It was time to decide since Hope and Libby were getting close to finishing high school.

"I'm applying to culinary school."

She blurt it out.

"Is that like college?" J.J. was the youngest of them and the furthest away from making that decision.

"Yeah, except it isn't. You essentially learn the job you want. The Culinary Institute of America is in New York State. That's my top pick."

"Ooh, cool. Yeah, I want to go to beauty school."

"It's not called that. It's called cosmetology. And you can do that while you're in high school, my high school has that anyway," Viv edified them.

"This is big news. Is your mother okay with culinary school?" Libby asked. Libby was headed to college too, name a ritzy one, and she could get in. Her grades and her parent's bank account would ensure that Libby could go just about anywhere.

"Well, seeing as I haven't told her, she's great with it," Hope said. She was sure her mother would have a total conniption.

"I'm skipping college altogether. Straight to Hollywood for me," Goldie announced.

"Why wouldn't you get a degree in fine arts, drama?" Libby questioned Goldie's plan.

"Because I will learn on the job. Do you think Farrah Fawcett has a drama degree? Or Demi Moore? No, they do not. Waste of time."

"You're going to need a backup. You should go to college, even in California," Libby said.

Goldie rolled her eyes at the suggestion. Goldie did have *Charlie's Angels'* good looks. But more Cheryl Ladd than Farrah, Hope thought.

"Well, your parents aren't going to have a conniption. Mine will," Hope said.

"Yeah, they will," Viv agreed.

But it was settled in Hope's mind. She loved cooking and baking, and she had seen every episode of the *Frugal Gourmet*. While the rest of the girls were obsessed with *General Hospital*, Hope was locked on PBS and *Everyday Cooking with Jacques*

Pepin. She'd watched her VHS tapes of Julia Child's *The Way to Cook* over and over and over. Thanks to her grandparents, she'd come to learn about fresh food, how to grow it, prepare it, and why it was so important to create with it!

Food was her calling. She knew it.

Goldie interrupted the deep thoughts about their careers with a sighting of floating hunks.

"Oh, look, those guys that came from Ann Arbor with Henry, is that their boat?"

The conversation about Hope's plan to thoroughly disappoint her parents was quickly abandoned as they were thoroughly distracted by a boat full of college guys.

Chapter Seven

Hope, Present Day

A victory party at the Stirling Las Vegas Grand was in the category of Things That Did Not Happen to Hope.

"Everyone was overwhelmingly nice. It's almost easy to forget that this isn't my actual life."

"Are you kidding? I just saw you actually win this entire food competition. Nothing pretend about it," Libby said.

"I'm in shock over that and other recent events. And I appreciate what you've done tonight; you made me seem much savvier about this stuff than I am."

Another agent had given Hope a business card and said something about a book. Hope's jaw dropped for the millionth time, and Libby Quinn saved the day.

"She's fielding several offers. We'll keep a hold of this," Libby said.

Hope tucked the card into her cellphone case. "I am not fielding several offers."

"You will be. This is a huge thing you just did. Besides, it's good for me to check out the competition."

"Competition for me? Stop. I'm not dropping everything and moving to Irish Hills." Hope did love the summers there; she hadn't been in a lake on a raft since.

Archie only liked swimming pools.

She did her best to be gracious, take pictures with the Best Dishes bigwig organizers, and she also hugged her fellow competitors.

Libby floated in and out, and if Hope hadn't just intercepted Archie, well, maybe it would have been an awesome night.

But he'd ruined it for her. From across the country, he'd ruined it.

Well, not completely. At one point, the famous Chef Rami Ellston oohed and aahed over her dish.

"I need the recipe, *need* it," Chef said.

Libby winked at Hope.

"How much do I owe you for making me look so good in front of my old friend here?" Hope said.

"Please, I've always known you were a rock star."

"Well, well, well, imagine seeing you here." A tall, handsome man appeared on the edge of the circle of their conversation and quickly took center stage.

He was dressed in a suit that likely cost the same as Hope's entire house.

"Imagine, are you having me followed these days?"

"Hardly. My name is on the building."

"Hard to miss that."

Libby seemed incredibly rude all of a sudden. What was this about?

"Do you know Chef Ellston?" the man said.

"We just met; will you excuse me? I think I need some fresh air," Libby said and abruptly left the little group.

"Stirling, I was just trying to steal this one's recipe," Chef Ellston said.

Hope was standing there with the owner of the hotel and celebrity chef Rami Ellston! She actually bit the inside of her cheek to be sure she hadn't slipped into a dream state!

"The key is the zucchini," she said. And felt like an idiot. The key to zucchini is the zucchini; yeah, brilliant commentary, Hope, brilliant.

"I'm sure it's delicious. I wonder, could I borrow Chef Ellston for a moment?"

"Of course," Hope said. She was glad to slip out of the orbit of the rich and famous. Time to say her good nights, thank Libby for being so sweet, and get back to her corner of nitty-gritty earth.

"You'll be the centerpiece," she heard Stirling Stone say to Chef Ellston.

It was time for a good night's sleep. This dose of glitter could really spoil her. And really, she was spoiling to hash it out with Archie. Maybe burn her duvet cover, disinfect their shower, you know, the glamorous life.

Hope's phone buzzed, and there it was: Archie. Presumably, just now seeing the colorful message she'd left him.

Hope walked out of the party and onto the balcony outside the banquet space.

The lights of Vegas twinkled in the horizon like stars. They weren't, though. She looked up, took a breath, and answered the call.

"What in the heck was that?"

"Hi, Archie."

"You send that picture to me, flipping me off? What kind of message is that?"

"Archie, do you realize we share a cloud on the iPad?"

"What?"

"I can see that new receptionist at the dealership is working out. That's who it is, right? She was butt naked, on our bed, on my duvet, actually. Looks like you're having the time of your life. I saw all those pictures."

"That is not your business. And it is not what you think."

"No, really? It's exactly what I think."

"Look, you're being very stupid."

It stung when he called her names. That was a favorite of his, telling her she was dumb. It hurt that the man who was supposed to love her could so easily be so mean to her with his words.

"I'm stupid, very nice."

"NO, I said you're *being* stupid."

"Ah, such a distinction. So, I know your big news, you're in a wonderfully playful relationship with uh, Bambi? I mean, I know it's not Bambi. That's just my pet name for her."

"Carla."

"Oh, okay, Bambi Carla. Don't you want to know my big news?"

"I want you to stop acting like you know anything about this. You don't. Carla understands me."

Classic. Her middle-aged husband was looking for a woman who understood him but also had the body of a yoga instructor.

"I understand you too, Archie. I understand you're embarrassing our family and me, and from the pictures, well, you're embarrassing yourself."

"You never treated me like you cared if I slept with someone else, so I finally did."

"Ah, sure, it's my fault." Hope wanted to throw the phone but realized Archie was too far away to hit.

"It is, in many ways, it's your fault. What am I supposed to do when you're in Vegas?"

Hope was tired of the conversation. Instead of apologizing, begging her forgiveness, or being ashamed, Archie was putting it all back on her. Like it was her fault that her husband was bored.

"You know what? You've got all the time you want now with

Bambi Carla. I'm not coming back from Vegas. You two can shack up day and night. Enjoy!"

"Really? What are you going to live on without my checkbook?"

That was a joke since Hope had paid her way out here with her catering jobs. She'd helped nearly pay off the mortgage and the girls' student loans. All with hard work, all because she thought they were a team. A dysfunctional team, but a team.

But they weren't. Maybe they never were.

"I won the whole thing, Archie. Did you hear that? I won the whole thing. So, I've got a little bit to play with. Didn't you see that big check? It was real. Well, sort of."

"You won. Uh, congrat—"

"—Save it. We're done." Hope clicked off her phone.

She felt a hot sting of tears in her eyes. Did she love Archie? Or was this just the sting of being made a fool of? Of being rejected. Years and years rolled over her. Had she wasted them with Archie?

Hope felt a hand on her arm.

Libby.

"Hey, can I help? Get you something?"

"I just told Archie I wasn't coming back. I have no idea what I'm going to do next. But I'm not going back there." She was trying not to cry, trying not to sob. But the words came out of her throat like coughs, each one ripped out of her lungs like bile.

"Come back to Irish Hills with me. I told you, I've got a cottage on the water rent-free, and I'm telling you, you'll fall in love with this little space downtown. It's made for you and for your talent with food."

"I can't promise anything. I don't have a culinary degree or business degree even. I've never even lived on my own or—" The things Hope hadn't done were piling up in her mind. That word regret popped in again.

She didn't want to live with any more of it.

"You don't have to promise anything," Libby reassured her. "How about we just go back and have a boat ride or two?"

"That is as good a plan as any." Tears started rolling down her face.

Libby moved forward and circled her in a hug. "It's okay, sis."

Hope felt her body shudder with the sobs she tried to hold in but couldn't.

Libby was quiet. She was strong. Hope leaned on Libby while the wave of anger, betrayal, disappointment, and just everything rolled through her body.

And then it passed.

The wave had overtaken her, but now she was calm. She'd swam past the breakwater, and it was calm.

Libby gave her a tissue.

"Some mess you found here. I mean, you're trusting me with a lot, and you don't know me, you don't know Marcia H. Venerable."

"I know Hope Benton, and I'm one hundred percent sure you do too."

Libby's eyes were clear. They held hands. Libby was a steady presence; she radiated strength, and her confidence flowed to Hope. They were so different, but they didn't start out that way. They started the same, or as close as two people can be, back when they were Sandbar Sisters. Libby was throwing Hope a life preserver. Hope need only grab on. Suddenly grabbing for the life preserver seemed a better option than clawing at Archie. Because that was the scenario she could see if she went back home to Covington.

"Okay, I'll do it. I'm not saying I'll do all this crazy restaurant stuff, but I'll come back with you. I need to clear my head without Archie. You still have a raft I can lounge on?"

"YES! I can't wait to tell J.J. She'll flip!"

"J.J., I miss her." Hope remembered her summer friends. She needed that sunshine for a few days. Vegas had sun, but you did everything you could to hide from it. You went to shows, casinos, or cabanas. At the lake, you basked in it. You let it heal you. That's what Hope needed.

"I have no doubt you'll fall in love with Irish Hills, just like I did. The town needs you. It needs all of us."

"Are you always this persistent?"

"Yes, it's part of my charm."

It was settled. Hope would go to the lake. She'd lick her wounds. She'd figure out who she was and who she wanted to be.

She'd deferred her plans for so many reasons over the years.

Her phone buzzed.

"Archie?"

"Yep."

Hope blocked his number. And showed it to Libby.

"There you go. Now, let's get out of Vegas, this dumb hotel, ugh, and back to the lake," said Libby. It was solid, definitive, more than anything Hope could come up with in this tumultuous moment. Though she thought the Stirling Grand was far from dumb. It was the swankiest place on the strip. Alas, Libby had moved in different circles than Hope.

Hope felt something was happening. A shift. It was more than just Archie's midlife crisis.

Several times in Hope's life, she could clearly see the fork in the road. She could look at it in the moment and realize, oh, here's where I change course.

Except the turns had always been left turns, unprotected, into oncoming traffic.

Maybe this time, it could be different.

Or she'd get hit by a bus.

Either way, she'd be done with Archie.

Chapter Eight

Hope

"I would not have figured you as a Jeep person," Hope said.

The ninety-minute drive from Detroit Metro Airport to Irish Hills gave Hope and Libby a chance to fill in some of the blanks of their lives.

It was decades of blanks. But Hope started to get a better picture.

She was feeling strange, untethered, and like a fool when it came to Archie. But Libby, who seemed so accomplished, so together, shared her own marital experience. It was a doozy.

It made Hope feel slightly less humiliated by the tumult she was in and less embarrassed that her old friend had reentered her life at this weird moment. If they were going to a planned reunion or something, Hope would have tried to present something better or shinier. She'd have painted a veneer on top of her real life to gloss it up for public consumption.

But her life was far from shiny right now. It was rusted and busted. Libby had witnessed it. There was no backpedaling. Libby saw Hope flip the bird to her husband and she'd spilled her guts about why.

"When Henry disappeared, he did so with just about every nickel I had. So, I sold the house, turned in the leased vehicles, all that. This Jeep was the kids' car when they lived with us. We'd paid cash. It was like the only thing I didn't owe on. I literally packed it with what I wanted to keep, drove here."

Hope imagined the scene and wondered if she was in her own similar one right now.

"So, explain to me, you're now the owner of Nora House, though? Your fortunes seemed to improve drastically. Not to be rude and talk money."

"It's okay, yeah, the house was a pre-inheritance. Aunt Emma can't take care of it. So she claims—she's healthy as a horse as far as I can see. Anyway, she also got us both into a real, uh, interesting position. Over the last year or so, she's bailed out any business that was struggling in Irish Hills, from the main downtown drag to the old dance pavilion. She had a sizeable amount of money as the last living direct heir of my great grandfather, Albert Libby."

"Ooh, the auto industry money, right? And wait how old IS Aunt Emma?"

"Born during the Depression, kind of amazing, right?"

"It's mind-boggling, and she's healthy?"

"Yeah, pretty much. Although, she's buying and buying and buying in Irish Hills to stave off Stirling Stone so that was unbalanced."

"Oh my, you mean the Stirling Stone of Stirling Grand?" Libby's iciness to the hotel owner made more sense all of a sudden.

"Yeah, that one. Anyway, she got in his way. She gummed up the works for his plans. Well, we did, once she got me on board."

"Now I know why you looked like you were smelling rotten eggs when Stone walked up."

"Ha, yeah, he keeps following my every move. Granted, I was in his casino, but still, he's the resources to spy on me."

"So, you stopped them from steamrolling Irish Hills with imminent domain?"

"Yes, pretty much, they go before the city council again in the fall. But the picture has changed drastically. You'll see. I can't wait for you to see it. Irish Hills is set to thrive!"

"You're going to make sure it does. I can see that."

"Ha, Stirling Stone doesn't like to lose. But I've learned that I love a challenge. And as you can see, this place is worth the fight." Libby nodded out the window, and Hope switched her focus from her old friend to the beauty of Irish Hills.

"Oh, wow, it's like being seventeen again," Hope said. She rolled down her window and inhaled. The lake! You could feel it in the air.

"There's something that just is summer to me here. It floored me too. Like no other place in my life." Libby paused for moment, letting Hope drink it all in. Then she added, "If you're up to it, I'm hoping to show you the restaurant space, then we can drive out to the cottage?"

Hope gave Libby a sidewise glance. She knew her friend was better than anyone at taking charge and making sure everyone fell in with her plans. Hope was here to take a few days off and enjoy the cottage while she licked her wounds. Libby's aim was to get Hope to commit to more.

"I'd love to see downtown, all your work, for sure. Yes. But you know I haven't said yes to this idea. I'm here for a break, not a business."

Libby was the Queen of Confidence; it was in her nature to tilt her chin into the wind and dare the world to try to stop her. It appears the world had come up short every time, and Libby had won every dare.

Hope felt like she used to be that way, that she used to be confident. However, she'd dared the world to stop her, and the world did.

Hope did always dream of a food life. Her best memories

growing up were here, with her friends at the lake or her grandparents learning about the food they grew.

Was this the time to open a new business? She had catering clients in Covington. She could build on that back home. Hope was only sure that she wasn't sure!

Seeing the building Libby had renovated wasn't making a promise. She wanted to see Libby's triumph. She wanted to be inspired by her old friend's accomplishments.

Libby drove toward town and described the project. "We've got five spaces to lease on the lakeside area of downtown. The structures are side by side. You'll remember, though, they're not like a strip mall. Each one is a unique space. At the end is the space we're turning into a restaurant. The roof, electricity, plumbing, heating, and cooling are all up to code. Dean Tucker, J.J.'s husband, has helped me replace, shore up, and repair everything we needed. He's my right-hand man. You'll love him. Oh, and we kept the historic charm but brought all the infrastructure into the twenty-first century."

"It sounds like you've been working your tail off."

"I have, but as you'll see, the restaurant space can be arranged your way. Your kitchen, your décor, your theme. Whatever you have ever dreamed of for your own place, you could do."

Hope shook her head. She tried to stop her brain. She knew exactly what she'd do but didn't say it. Libby was clearly able to take even the smallest kernel of an idea and run with it. Hope wasn't ready to give her old friend an inch on this because it was easy to see Libby had the mile ready to go.

"Here we are," Libby said.

Downtown Irish Hills was the same and also different. The center gazebo was under repair, scaffolding was set up, and caution tape blocked the entrance.

"How many ice cream cones did we eat on those benches in there?" Hope said as the memory of their bikes propped on the side of the gazebo flashed into her mind.

"We kept the character of the old one and the details, but we're making it larger and connected to power for a sound system. It's set to be completed next week."

Hope looked across the street to a stretch of buildings that were crumbling, boarded, and straight-up depressing.

Libby followed her eyeline and grimaced. "Yeah, that's phase two. I'm working on that. But this side, this side is almost ready for you!" She nodded her head to the lakeside stretch of buildings.

"You're terrible," Hope said.

They pulled up to the parking space.

"Yes, one hundred percent terrible."

Hope got out of the Jeep and looked up and down the little stretch of small-town perfection.

"You're kidding, right? This can't be real."

The five buildings were a part of a row, that much Libby had said. What she hadn't described was just how each had a distinct character. Each its own color, one with natural red brick, the next painted white, one ornate, adjacent to another with a plainer architectural style. There was a three-story space in the center, bookended by two-story neighbors. The end buildings were larger and l-shaped so they could turn the corners, giving them two window banks adjacent to the sidewalk.

Just beyond the end of the row, a lane stretched straight down to the lake.

The proximity of the lake made this hamlet feel more like Nantucket than Southern Michigan. In the distance, the water reflected the clear blue sky and twinkled with sunlight.

Hope took it in. The armor she'd put up against being sucked in by Libby's plan took a hit. The water and the building made her see Irish Hills through Libby's eyes.

"We did everything we could to keep the old feel but also be a great partner for businesses interested in these spaces," Libby said.

"Nailed it," Hope remarked.

"Thank you, we have a lot to do. The tornado crippled the town we used to know."

"Wow, people never rebuilt from '89?" Hope remembered the dark funnel barreling toward them that long-ago summer day.

"Yes, a lot of people and businesses didn't bounce back."

Speaking of tornadoes, a petite woman with dark hair in a shag cut and a voice Hope hadn't heard in decades burst out the front door of the proposed restaurant space.

"HOPE!!!!"

J.J. Pawlak was a dynamo in a completely different way than Libby. She was energy, mirth, and laughter, all compressed into a petite package.

Hope felt tears spring to her eyes.

"J.J.!" The two women hugged hard, and then Hope stepped back to get a better look.

"How in the world can you look fifteen? Aren't we fifty?"

"That we are," said Libby.

"It's all the green juicing I do."

"A margarita is not green juice," said Libby.

"A margarita does too qualify as green juice. Lime is squeezed. Juice is had. It's health food."

Hope laughed and felt her younger self take a step forward over the broken glass of her current life. Who knew laughing with old friends was a time machine, no matter how long it had been?

"I'm about to wow Hope with Dean's work. He's turned these spaces into one of a kind gems," Libby said.

"Oh, please don't tell him that. He'll insist I make dinner or something ridiculous."

A burly man in a Tucker Contractor t-shirt with a tool belt, a salt and pepper beard, and a big smile walked out the door next.

Hope assumed it was Dean himself. He towered over his petite wife. But the same energy radiated from him as it did J.J.

"I heard that! And give me a break. I deserve a reward for this building, not an act of violence in a casserole dish." The affection in his eyes when he criticized his wife's cooking was clear. The comment was sweet, not nasty.

Hope had a little spike of envy. Why couldn't Archie be more like that? His idea of banter was calling her stupid.

She shook it off. Archie could be any way he wanted. He was back in Kentucky having his midlife crisis or whatever.

"This is Hope. One of the ladies from the eighties," J.J. said.

"Hope is a chef," Libby added.

"Home cook and caterer," Hope corrected. She didn't want to make them think she was more than she was. She was no chef; she hadn't earned that title. She managed a breakfast diner at best and didn't run the kitchen at all.

"Fine, Hope just won a huge title, The Best Cook in the World, but she's not a chef."

"Stop," Hope said.

"Wow! You won the whole thing? That's so great!!" J.J. high-fived her.

It was sweet, they hadn't seen each other in forever, but she felt affection and love from J.J. and Libby as if they'd never parted.

She also felt bad that she didn't know a thing about the two women who had swept in and swept her up. She'd figured out that Libby was a powerhouse community organizer. Get it done, society, bigwig, the kind of woman that might have intimidated the heck out of Hope back in her PTA days.

J.J. owned a salon or worked at a salon. The last few hours had been a whirlwind. A million new details about her life, and her friends, were trying to sort themselves.

Dean took over the sales pitch.

"Well, when you give the tour, we've laid it out so you can set up the kitchen your way. The storeroom is fixed, the cooler there also installed and set. But the shelving can be configured any way you'd like. We've got an awning coming in here for covered seating, and it will extend around that corner. A patio is about to be poured. You'll have space for outdoor tables, even pods if you need, for the next global crisis."

"Wow, you've got the jump on a lot of what a restauranteur would ask for," Hope said. She had friends who were chefs. It was her world or her world adjacent. And they were all keeping an eye out for outdoor spaces and safe dining options after what the last few years had been like.

"That's our fearless leader here. She's very specific," Dean said.

Libby shook her head. "Thank you, it comes down to being smart enough to find great people, that's it. Now, let's go on in," Libby said.

Hope watched Libby graciously take a compliment. Hope was used to fighting compliments. Why didn't she just say thank you like Libby did? Libby likely got a lot of compliments based on what Hope could see she had accomplished in her life. This was just one project. Wow. That was all Hope could think: Wow.

"This is all Lincoln Brick Factory stuff, and they went out of business in 1947, so we did have to do a little matching and patching. Got super lucky at a salvage yard, picked up everything they had."

Hope looked at the weathered brick exterior that Dean described. "You did a great job. I can't see any difference," she said.

The door to the restaurant space was painted black. There were two large windows, with black panes on the street side and the corner side.

"I've ordered a black-and-white stripe for the awning, but that can change, say the word."

Libby went in first. Hope decided not to point out that she hadn't agreed to opening a restaurant here. She hadn't agreed to anything but a few days of rest at the lake. Yet somehow, as the doors opened and they walked into the space, her dreams became real.

The place was beautiful. Dean had left the brick on the interior walls exposed. There was an old painted mural on one wall. There were exposed ducts and beams. It was too good to be true, as if Hope's dreams had somehow traveled through the air to this place and became solid.

On one wall, in black and white, was a message painted into the brick: *Premium Quality Fine Dining, Fresh and Tasty, Best in Town.*

"Aunt Emma said this was on the wall of the old restaurant," Dean said. "It predates you ladies, from the eighties, by a good bit. We found it when we removed drywall. Maybe it's 1930s or so. I thought it was cool, but again, if it's not your vision..."

"This can't be real." Hope stepped forward and ran her finger along the edge of the sign.

Hope looked at Libby. She wanted to say, "Yes, I want this. I want to build my dream right here. That sign, this place, this vibe."

But she stopped. This was madness. Hope needed to think, to plan, but she was honest. There was no denying they'd done an amazing job with this place.

"Your instincts were spot on," she said instead. "It's authentic, cool, I love it."

Hope looked up. The ceiling was two stories high, with metal beams, also exposed but painted a deep red.

"There's a suite of rooms up, sort of off the back of the second story. You can use some for offices, but for the main dining room we wanted to go with this open feel."

Hope didn't say a word. She just looked up and felt what Libby had intended, that this space was just right, somehow.

And then she looked down and dropped down to her knees. She ran her fingers over the floor. It looked like distressed cobblestone, but it was smooth.

"Painted concrete?"

"This is a great option to give us that old-time charm, but you can literally hose it down if needed," Dean explained.

"It's stunning." There wasn't a wrong step in the space. Hope could imagine the layout, with round tables in the center and larger ones on the four corners. Wait, what? She wasn't moving in. It was just a tour.

"We envisioned the hostess station here." Libby pointed out a good spot to the right of the front door.

"We need someone good. I have a person in mind, she might be perfect, anyway, just my two cents," J.J. chimed in as they walked further into the space.

"We've got about three-thousand square feet to play with on the main floor. Upstairs there's space that could be a banquet area."

Libby could have been a real estate agent, Hope thought, as her friend outlined the specs.

Hope calculated the numbers.

"Using sixty-forty, that would mean we could serve about one hundred people in the main space, figuring eighteen-square feet per person, unless it's more casual, then maybe more," Hope said, without thinking about how it sounded.

"Aha, got her," J.J. said. And Libby shot J.J. a satisfied look.

"No, no, just doing math."

"You said 'we,'" J.J. pointed out.

"Let's go look at the space for the kitchen." Libby clearly didn't want to stop the vibe or interrupt the current delusions swirling around Hope's brain.

She *had* just said 'we.' Her mind had already decided the square footage per diner. What was happening?

They walked through the dining area. A bar separated the main dining area from a space that looked ready for a range and ovens.

"We could wall this off, but the bar was already here. Dean said there are options."

"It looks perfect, don't change a thing." This was a command, a decision about a space that she had zero claim on. It was as if her brain was moving in already, envisioning this restaurant, her restaurant.

Hope moved forward without her two old friends. She could see the range, even though it wasn't there. She imagined people sitting at the bar as she cooked. She looked up. There needed to be hanging lights here and a pot rack.

She moved in a circle, looked back over the dining room again, and then back to the endless soapstone counter. Her hand ran along the cool surface. They'd plate here, in full view of the diners. The diners would be a part of the experience.

Hope looked. There were two doors on either side of the massive wall that would house the range and oven.

Perfect for flow, one in and one out.

She pushed one open and walked back to the kitchen space. She noticed a cooler and dozens of shelves for dishware above more counters, but these were stainless steel. There was also a commercial mixer.

There were several huge sinks, and a commercial dishwasher was already installed.

Libby and Dean had thought of everything. Everything.

There was a door that led to a stairwell, which must be to the upstairs banquet space.

She was about to go up, but then the back door caught her eye.

The window in the door revealed how close they were to the lake.

Hope walked out the back. There were a few parking spaces, then she rounded the corner to see the spot that would be the outdoor patio.

In the distance, the lake glistened. They weren't on the lake, exactly. It was still maybe one eighth of a mile away. But you could see it. You could see it from the patio space.

"Wow. Just wow."

Libby and J.J. joined her outside.

"So, what do you want to call it?" J.J. asked.

Hope snapped out of it. She wasn't moving to Irish Hills and opening a restaurant! That was ridiculous! She was a housewife from Kentucky who dabbled in food. Archie's voice rang in her ears. This was a hobby. She didn't have what it took to make this dream happen.

"I, uh, I need to pump the breaks."

"It's okay. I just wanted you to see it. I know that there's something here that could be spectacular with the right partner," Libby said. Her tone was gentle. Her old friend had caught Hope's fear and doubt. She softened her sales pitch.

"It's beautiful," Hope said. "You all did a wonderful job...but you don't need me. You need someone who knows what they're doing. I think it's beautiful enough you could get a celebrity chef on board, seriously."

"Hmm, well, maybe that's enough for one day. I know my plans can be a lot. I bet you need some toes in the sand time," Libby said.

"I do, yes, thank you." Hope had to get her head straight. Her life was in ruins. Standing here fantasizing about becoming a real chef? Well, that was juvenile. That was denial in the face of her current situation.

"Catch up with me. We'll have a drink or two this weekend." J.J. said her goodbyes.

Libby and Hope got back in the Jeep, where the second phase of the charming lake offensive would nearly do Hope in.

Chapter Nine

Hope

"Your generosity, it's too much."

Libby had driven them to Orchard Beach Drive. The place was three houses from the corner of Cottage and Orchard Beach and a mere two blocks away from Nora House on Sandy Beach Lane.

Hope looked at it and blurted out, "You gotta be kidding me!"

"Ha, cute, right? It was built in the early fifties, according to Aunt Emma. I haven't had time to check."

The little cottage had a center door with a window on each side, and flower boxes stretched the width of them, though no one had planted anything in them. The siding was a faded yellow and the door, chipped as it was, was still a welcoming green color.

"Don't look at the paint. It needs to be stripped and redone."

Hope listened but disagreed. It was tiny perfection.

"Who owned it before you got it?

"Back in our day, it was a family from Toledo worked at the Jeep plant, Emma said. Anyway, their kids moved out to Oregon and didn't visit here. Sold it to Emma. She was convinced this was a prime spot, and well, she is right. The beach here is sandy, with easy lake access, sunsets, and the works. Even though the cottage is only eight hundred square feet."

The cottage's kitchen and living space were open to each other. There was a brick fireplace, a little table, chairs, a slipcovered love seat, and Hope was drawn to the vintage refrigerator.

"This is a vintage GE Deluxe! I mean, I'm dying!"

"Right? It works."

"It's all spruced up. Did you know I would come?"

"I just did," Libby said. "Stove works too. No idea about that old Tappan oven."

"Well, I don't plan to bake here. I plan to bake out there." Hope said and pointed to the lake.

"Well, there are three tiny bedrooms, one bathroom—ignore the pink tile—and there's a shed out back. Not sure what's in there. I've barely gotten to my own shed at Nora House."

"You're incredible. I mean, taking all this on?"

"I don't know how to explain it, but I needed this as much as it needed me," Libby said.

She looked happy, and while she was clearly motivated and energized, she didn't seem desperate. Vitality. That was the word. Libby Quinn radiated with vitality for life and this project she was pitching.

The best part was the last part. The little place was right on the water. Hope looked out the row of windows. They needed washing, no doubt, but the lake was the star of the show. Each window framed the lake, only a few feet away, out back.

"This place is clean, has all the basics, kitchen, linens, bed, chair, sofa, but it's kind of bare-bones. No one has been in it for a while. My aunt had renters at one point, but then she couldn't remember her VRBO password. It was a whole thing."

"I can pay. Let me pay."

"You are doing me the favor of being here, so no."

Hope put down her bags. She was suddenly incredibly tired.

The last few days started to press on her shoulders like a physical weight.

"Look, J.J. also stocked some food in the little fridge. You can just rest, chill, the water is warming up, so take a swim. I'm just down the road, walking distance."

"I remember the way. Thank you, I am tired. I think I could sleep a bit."

"Do what you need to, text me tomorrow, and I'm at your service—oh and so is the truck. Hold on, I better be sure of that." Libby walked over to a side door and opened it. "Yep, it's there."

Hope looked over her shoulder, and there it was, a pickup truck, vintage too, by the looks of it. It reminded her of her Grandpa Benton's old truck.

"It's not fancy, but it works. I promise. Keys are in the top drawer there. I've learned Uber isn't exactly a thing out here."

"It's more than I need right now."

"I know we pushed a little hard today, and I'm sorry for that. You deserve time to decompress. Just keep an open mind, though. This could be the place. Turned out it is for me."

"Got it, I'll think about it. After I pass out for a bit."

Libby stepped forward and hugged Hope. "Rest up. I'm sure there are margaritas ala J.J. in our future. As soon as you're settled."

"Oh boy, thanks for the warning."

Libby left Hope alone in the little cottage. It felt familiar to Hope. It felt like her summers here. It felt like a time before life was so seriously adult.

Archie and her kids had never been here. She felt sad at that. It was an opportunity lost. Her girls might have liked it.

Hope opened a few windows, and the slightly musty lake smell aired out quickly. She walked the space. It was more than enough for her for a few days.

She didn't know how many days she was going to even be here, really. She had cleared her schedule of catering jobs, thanks to her trip to Vegas. But still, she couldn't just abandon her real-life forever. She'd have to deal with it.

Hope looked in the vintage fridge. Milk, cheese, eggs, and some bottled water. There was a chilled can of Pillsbury crescent rolls, butter, and a few other staples in the cabinets. An elegant sufficiency, that was what her grandpa used to say. There was an elegant sufficiency of food and accommodations for her for a few days of peace.

She stared at the can of crescent rolls in a tube. It was a doughy little timebomb. She jumped every time she popped one open, even now.

That pressurized tube was a metaphor for her current life. The time bomb of her marriage had finally popped like that can of rolls. Now each part of her life was being pulled apart. The sticky ends were separating at the rough perforations.

She believed wholeheartedly that Archie could kiss her butt. He didn't deserve a check-in from her or anything else right now. But her kids. She probably should call the girls. She had texted them she won when she boarded a flight for Michigan and had received appropriate emoji responses.

Maybe she'd try again with a call after a little soak of her feet in the lake?

Hope's suitcase was packed with clothes she wanted to cook in, not vacation in. She pondered what to do about a swimsuit.

She had a lot to ponder.

Had she left Archie? For good? The rest of her clothes, her mementos of the kids, and her favorite mixer, were all still in their Covington house. She really only cared about the mixer and the pictures. Did she need to talk to a lawyer next?

Did she need to get a moving company? What did people do?

What Hope did have was one hundred eight thousand dollars in cash. And an honest picture of her marriage.

Hope walked out back toward the old dock. The wooden slats

creaked as she put her feet down. The planks were dry and rough on her bare feet. But it felt good. It felt familiar.

Though it was old, it seemed solid enough. She walked out to the end. There was a little boat, covered with a tarp, clipped to the side. She wondered what else might be around for her to use to enjoy the lake.

But for now, the sun, and the water, that was all she needed. She needed it more than she realized.

Hope sat down on the edge and plunged her feet in.

Whoa!!!

It was cold. Libby had said the water was warming up, but there was still a chill. It was June, and the sun was blazing this afternoon. And soon, her skin adjusted to the temperature.

The cool water felt good. She imagined what a little luxury it would be, after running her restaurant, to soak her tootsies at the end of the night.

No, this was not good. This thinking she could do whatever she wanted. This investing in the idea that her dreams could come true.

She'd been down this road before.

Chapter Ten

Hope, 1990

It was a scene.

"This is not fair." Hope was nearly yelling. She never yelled at her mother. Her mother did the yelling. Her father was quiet.

He was no ally. He did what Mother wanted. Whatever that was, without question. Placating Mother was his full-time job.

She was expected to do the same.

"We will not pay for culinary school. Period. That is not a path to a stable career, health benefits, nothing. You will wind up waitressing. You have good SAT scores and excellent PSAT scores. And you want to waitress?"

"There is nothing wrong with waitressing, number one. Number two, I want to be the chef. I want to run a restaurant. It's completely different." She'd applied and been accepted to the Culinary Institute of America in New York. It was no small feat, getting in, and she'd done it!

"Oh, listen to her, Perry. She's going to run the restaurant."

Her mother made Hope sound like she was an idiot. A child.

"You just said I had good test scores. I'm smart enough to do what I want to do as a career."

"But too stupid to know you're being ridiculous. How many tips do you think you need to earn to cover culinary school out of state and rent? Oh, and how are you going to get to New York, the car? Because that car your dad bought is staying here. Perry, your daughter, is playing pretend."

Her dad had said it was a birthday present. Her parents had never once even driven in it. But now, it wasn't hers the minute she tried to strike out independently with it.

Her mother was mean, straight-up mean. She was using everything she could think of to control Hope. She always had.

"Honey, the University of Cincinnati is very nice. We met there."

Her father was trying to smooth it all out. To mollify her mother. He was going to light his pipe now. His stupid pipe. He could fiddle with that and ignore everything else.

As she predicted, he did just that. It was over. It was settled. She didn't have a thing against the University of Cincinnati, except it wasn't what she wanted to do.

She had no ally.

"Fine. Fine. I'll wear what you say, go get the degree you say, say what you say, and have a boring, stupid life just like yours."

It was harsh, Hope knew, but she was livid.

"So dramatic. Perry, someone better warn Meryl Streep. The best actress of the year is in our rec room."

Her mother was mocking her. She couldn't be in the room with her for another minute.

She ran up to her bedroom. She was going to slam her bedroom door. But she knew that would mean her mother would run up here after her. She'd hammer away at Hope until she got the last word.

No, she didn't slam the door. She shut it. Quietly. She balled her fists until her arms shook. Hope felt pent-up anger. There was a fight in her that had nowhere to land. She knew, in a fight, her mother would win. Her mother was the master, Hope, the obedient puppet.

She looked around her room. She wanted to rip down the INXS poster, knock over her stupid Caboodle, and pull down the balloon valance over her window. She wanted to tear the place up.

But Michael Hutchence didn't deserve her wrath.

Her powder blue phone sat on her nightstand. Aha! She'd act out her rebellion with a phone call.

She crawled over her bed and picked up the receiver. She watched as the dial rotated back. Over and over and over.

"Hey, hi. Can you pick me up?"

"At your house?"

"Actually, no." Hope gave him a different address. Archie Venerable was an escape hatch. Her parents hated his guts, he was rough, a little crude, and they thought he was 'on drugs.'

He was mostly smoking pot, though. So, it was just enough of the wild side for Hope without being a total burnout.

She'd go out with Archie tonight and blow off steam. She just had to wait out her parents a little. They would be sure they'd won, and the argument was over.

Her parents were in the den watching some Civil War documentary. They'd fall asleep without fail during that thing. By the time they did, it was dark. And it was time for her to go.

Hope slid her window open and then pulled the screen gently into her room. Her parents were clueless about how she snuck out of the house. Her room was on the second floor. But there was a little overhang over the bay window below. It was wide enough to stand on. She climbed out and steadied herself on it. She leaned over to be sure they weren't standing at the window. Unlikely, but best to check. The coast was clear.

She used her arms to hang down and then dropped the few feet to the grass. She landed on her backside with a thud. She was still for a second, but no one inside had heard her land.

Hope dusted herself off. And stood up straight. Archie was going to pick her up one block over. She adjusted her attitude and her purse across her shoulder.

See if they could control her now! She ran down the block and over to where she'd told him to meet her.

Archie was there, looking dangerous. He had a cool car, a cool-looking cigarette, and a Johnny Depp vibe. She could work with it.

"Hey," he said as he leaned over to push open the passenger side door.

"Hey."

"Get in."

Hope looked back down the street. Take that, Mother. You may be able to crush this dream of mine, but you don't know everything, do you?

Hope's life did change that night.

Drastically. And it had nothing to do with her mother's plan.

Chapter Eleven

Libby, Present Day

It had gone well with Hope. Libby couldn't have predicted the state of Hope's marriage, but still, her old friend had won that entire cooking contest.

Hope was at a crossroads like Libby had been. Maybe this was the fates aligning.

They had lately, for Libby. Except for one area, her kids. She wished they'd check in more often. This was summer at the lake; she had a ton of room. Surely, they could all find a week, or a long weekend, and visit. She hated to hope too much for that.

She knew she needed to be happy without them in her day-to-day life. But still, every time she went on a boat ride or, more recently, wiped out while trying to stay upright after dropping one ski, she thought, *the kids would love this*.

She stood out on her dock at sunset. Tonight, it was orange and pink. Other nights it was blue and gray. Still, other nights, it was a faded blue. Bradley, the Great Blue Heron, skimmed across the water.

"Hey, Bradley." She had named him Bradley. He seemed fine with it. She snapped a pic of Bradley. Libby sent the pic in a group chat to her three kids.

She didn't expect them to uproot their lives or anything, but maybe, if she kept slowly showing them how great it was here at Nora House, she'd get them out for a visit.

She'd keep working on them, little by little.

She was needed here; she was doing something important. Her kids weren't responsible for keeping her busy or happy. That was her gift to them, she knew.

The list of things she had to do for Irish Hills was long. Too long, but she'd been having the time of her life checking things off as they accomplished them. 'They' was the key word.

Dean, J.J., and Keith had been her squad! They'd helped her each step of the way, from Dean's skills to J.J's upbeat belief that this would work, to Keith's, well. Somehow, she'd fallen into a romance with her old boyfriend.

This thought continued to make her blush and made her believe that there were second chances when you least expected them.

The unmistakable sound of tires crunching the gravel of her driveway interrupted her thoughts. She wasn't expecting anyone. She was bushed after the whirlwind of heading out to Vegas and back. J.J. and Libby wanted to sit with Hope and reconnect over a glass of wine, but that could wait a day or two.

Libby walked back to the house and through to the drive side. She'd taken to thinking of the front door as the drive side and the back door as the lakeside. The front door opened to the driveway and any guests that pulled up. But it really felt like the back of the house since every inch of Nora House was designed to face the lake.

Libby opened the door to see a black SUV slowing to a stop.

Who in the world?

She put her hands on her hips as it dawned on her. She was

sure he'd been tipped off as to why she'd attended the cooking competition and reception at his hotel. Why did it have to be his hotel?

Stirling Stone's expensive leather loafer landed on the gravel of her driveway. It wasn't a good surface to walk on if you wanted to keep your fancy shoes fancy.

Stone was reportedly nearly as rich as Buffet, and Libby had decided to get in his way. Usually, she was asking his caliber of person for donations, not fighting them. It seemed like everywhere she went, he was there—or his lawyer was there.

So far, Stone had lost his bid to enact imminent domain and failed to remove Libby by luring her away with a great job in New York. She knew men like him did not like to lose and had the resources to keep fighting until they got what they wanted.

"I could have offered you a ride in my private jet. A shame you flew back here commercial."

"A shame. What do I owe the honor of this impromptu visit?"

Stone was polite and handsome, and it was easy to see why the silver fox, with impeccable grooming, was always on the eligible bachelor lists. A billion-dollar bank account didn't hurt either.

"Ms. Quinn, I apologize for dropping in without notice." Stirling Stone's eyes scanned Nora House.

She knew it was beautiful, not just the building but also the land. Nora House was built on a little peninsula, so it had water views on three sides.

"Yeah, it's a nice place," Libby said. "Another reason I'm working to save Irish Hills."

"I was told the best house on the lake was yours. It certainly is."

"Built by my great-grandfather. Did you want to go water skiing or something?"

"I just wanted to let you know, following your example of community service, I helped a charming town's efforts at revitalization."

"Oh?"

"Covert Pier, right on Lake Michigan, maybe you've heard of it?"

Stirling Stone knew full well she had heard of Covert Pier. They were two hours west. Covert Pier was her direct competition for the downtown development grant money. They wanted that five hundred thousand in town improvement money just as much as Irish Hills did.

And they were formidable. Covert Pier's plans were further along. They wanted to turn Covert Pier into the Traverse City of Southern Michigan.

"So, what did you do for Covert Pier?" Libby tried hard not to show any emotion. Stirling Stone was here to see how to ruffle her feathers.

"Yes, Covert Pier is really well positioned. No tornado damage either, which is nice. That's a real hurdle for you. Also, it's an easy drive from Chicago or South Bend, so that's a win too."

"Look, I'm sure it's very nice. But despite that, we're going to win the grant. I'm quite sure."

"Oh, yes, your friend the homemaker...funny to run into you in Vegas."

"Yeah, funny."

Stone was watching her every move. That was clear. He hadn't become the King of the Mountain accidentally.

"I know you need that grant money to finish all the renovations. And it is looking like a long shot for Irish Hills. I know your aunt's funds are running dry. Why don't you just sell it to me? I'll take care of it. Heck, I'd even put an offer in on this place. I love it."

"Our funds are just fine, and we have a great restaurant concept just about to sign on the dotted line ourselves, but I appreciate your concern."

"Look, I don't want to fight you. There are so many opportunities in my organization. You could help me rebuild this area. You could help manage my properties here."

"I know it was you who tried to lure me to that job in Manhattan. I got a great night in the city out of it, so thank you for that. But I've found my groove right here. I think I can do the most good right where I am."

"So, when will this restaurant of yours be opening?"

"I uh, that information isn't public yet. Rest assured, it's on a fast track." Libby was now lying through her teeth to Stirling Stone.

Hope was not convinced of the idea of opening a restaurant. And if she said no? Libby wasn't prepared with a solid backup plan. But she gave Stone a confident stare, nonetheless.

"Well, I'd like to invite you to the grand opening of Ellston's at the Pier. Celebrity Chef Rami Ellston will be opening his flagship restaurant on July 3rd. The grant committee will also be there."

"I thought Applebee's was committed to that space?" Libby had read Covert Pier's proposal. Applebee's was clearly in the plan.

"Yes, they were. But after talking with Chef Ellston in Vegas and telling him about the potential, well, it all fell into place. He's going pretty high-end. Honestly, Rami is the next Emeril or Wolfgang. He's going to do a restaurant concept at the Stirling Grand too."

Libby saw the writing on the wall. She might not have been lured by Stone's big money, but most would be. Stirling Stone had seen how she was trying to find a chef to open a restaurant, and he'd one-upped her.

"How wonderful for him. Thanks for the invite."

"You're welcome. I was in town and just thought I'd be sure you knew you'd be an honored guest at Ellston's on the Pier opening night."

While Libby was working to convince a reluctant and bruised Hope, Stone was throwing money at a superstar, super-confident, big-name chef.

"Thanks, but I'll be pretty busy here that week." She smiled and tried to look confident that her plans were all set too.

"Well, the offer's open if any of your plans fall through."

Libby did not reply.

Stone nodded and went back to his car. She watched as he drove away. Stone wanted her to quit, and seeing how she had won, so far, at every turn, he was trying new tactics. She was infuriated.

Libby was also in a panic. This tightened their time frame. The entire house of cards could collapse if she didn't get commitments for the buildings downtown. Hope just had to do the restaurant, and it had to be amazing.

With the five hundred thousand dollars, they could finish the renovations on the buildings on the lakeside and think about the strip across the street. If they did that, Stirling Stone would have zero case to make for tearing down Irish Hills. Zero.

If they failed, well, she knew that business owners here were struggling. Stone would be able to convince the town council that his plan was a windfall for them.

A familiar sound from the lake diverted her spiraling panic.

She walked around back and broke into a little run to get to her dock. Keith was there, with his baby, a lovingly restored 1966 Chris-Craft.

It was a welcome sight, and she grabbed the line and helped him softly dock.

"Q, looking gorgeous as usual."

"What?" Libby barely heard him. Her mind was occupied with the realization that Stone was putting up new obstacles to her plan. "Sorry, K. And that's sweet. Thank you."

"What's wrong?" Keith took her hand in his.

"I just had an unwelcome and aggressive visitor."

"What? Are you okay? Where?"

"No, no, I mean Stirling Stone, he was here to let me know how he's going to sabotage our grant proposal."

"Wow, so what's his evil plan?"

"He's recruited Rami Ellston to open a restaurant in Covert Pier."

"Well, great for them."

"It means they could win the grant money."

"So that's the reason you look like you could spit nails?"

"It is, yes. I have a million renovations to do, we need that money, and I have to convince a reluctant chef to open a restaurant in a few short weeks. And while that's happening, I have to figure out how to convince additional, viable businesses to commit to opening in a space that isn't fully renovated yet, that has no foot traffic because the town is dying, while also managing to be a good steward to Nora House or my crazy aunt will do something else crazy, and—"

In a move too fast to defend or even register with her human eyes, Libby was off her feet and over Keith's shoulder.

"—Hey, put me down!! You'll throw out your back."

Keith was fit and muscular but hoisting her over his shoulder wasn't smart.

"We're going on an evening dinner cruise for two."

He carefully plopped Libby down on the boat and started untying the line.

"I don't have time for cruising around. Did you just hear that list? And that's not all of it."

Keith stepped onboard. His weight caused the boat to bob on the water, and Libby fell into the chair next to the captain.

"Are you kidnapping me here?"

"Yes, for an hour. You sit and enjoy the water. There's a mini-bottle of wine in the cup holder, and I've got dinner in the cooler."

"Wow, dinner?"

"Well, it's all finger food, cheese, crackers, and stuff, but yes." Keith positioned himself at the wheel.

Libby's urge to protest and get back to worrying about her current slate of problems receded.

This was right. This was an hour of enjoying the moment. She'd forgotten to do that for the first part of her adult life. Now that she was in her fifties, she was going to learn from that mistake. Right now, the water was clear, the air was warm, the wine was chilled, and a handsome man was wooing her with delicious cheeses.

She was now smart enough to know that this present was a gift. "You had me at free cheese."

Keith leaned over; he gave her a gentle kiss. "Now, sit back, unwind, and don't backseat drive."

They pulled out into Lake Manitou.

"Don't go too fast," Libby said, ignoring the backseat driver's comment.

"What did I just say?"

"I just want this cruise to last longer than an hour."

Keith flashed a devastatingly handsome smile at her.

She spent the rest of the night not worrying.

She had tomorrow to convince Hope.

She'd figure it out. And she had help.

Stirling Stone was playing hardball, but Libby had moves too. Tomorrow she'd start playing her own game.

Chapter Twelve

Hope

Hope woke up late. She never slept in, never! For a moment, she worried that she was late for the kids or late for a job, or just late.

When was the last time Hope wasn't on someone else's schedule?

Then she remembered where she was. The breeze gently blew the curtains into the bedroom she'd selected. There were two more, but this was the largest and the only one with the window facing the water.

She sat up and looked outside. What time was it?

Hope realized she wasn't late for anything currently.

She was here to hide for a day or two and then figure out the rest of her life. Ha, no pressure.

It was going to be a good day, weather-wise. The sun was bright in the blue sky.

The idea of laying out flashed into her mind.

In her teens, baby oil, lemon juice, and no care in the world about sunscreen marked her days here on Lake Manitou.

Her grandparents' farm was long sold. They used to rent a cottage similar to this one for the Fourth. All the family would come. The Bentons didn't have Libby Quinn's pedigree or property, but they too had a history here.

Her father had moved to Ohio out of high school, but he let her come to Lake Manitou every summer. As long as she got a summer job here, she was allowed to stay on her grandparents' farm all summer.

Of course, she worked the farmstand when she was too young to work anywhere else. That was how she met Libby. Libby had ridden her bike over and filled a brown bag full of peaches.

They hit it off right away.

Growing up, she worked all over the Irish Hills. One summer, she was a beer cart girl at the golf course. Another summer, she scooped ice cream at Tut's, and her last summer here, she worked as a line cook for the breakfast shift at the old Lakeside Hotel.

That was the best one, the last one. That's where she'd made up her mind about her future.

Ha, that hadn't gone to plan.

They were all part-time jobs. When she wasn't working, it was Sandbar Sister time. They'd laid out on the sandbar or on the pontoon for literally six hours at a stretch. They didn't know that time was the luxury, not a boat or a house. Time to spend with each other just being was the luxury they had as kids.

Alright, that's it, Hope thought.

The last time she swam in this lake, she didn't know she wouldn't do it again for thirty years. She hadn't brought a swimsuit to Vegas. That was a work trip. But here she was on a gorgeous June morning at the lake of her youth.

Hope has rocked a bikini back in her younger days but hadn't worn one since the girls were born. The flat stomach of her eighteen-year-old self had gotten so stretched out during her first pregnancy that purple lines traveled across her abdomen like little road maps.

No amount of Windsor Pilates, which she loved back in the day, removed stretch marks. Hope had taken to hiding them after Archie had teased her about them.

No, no more two pieces for her.

Though, here, who would see?

Hope's sports bra and underwear would have to do. She grabbed a beach towel from the linen closet. Libby and J.J. had thoughtfully provided so many things here. The cottage was worn down, but it was clean, and thanks to her friends' attention to detail, any basic Hope needed, she found.

She walked down to the dock. The wood planks of the dock were hot, even though it was still morning. She should have brought flip-flops.

Well, the solution was easy. She put the towel on the edge of the dock and sat down. She'd gotten her feet wet yesterday, she wanted more today.

Hope took a quick look around. Was there anyone close enough to this dock and stretch of water to see and be traumatized by her naked stomach or lack of a proper swimsuit?

There was a cottage a few yards away, but no one was there that she could see. It felt pretty private, and it was early still. She realized no one cared, and nor was anyone on the lookout for a fifty-year-old woman's stretch marks.

Oh heck, what are you waiting for, Hope?

She stood up and stepped back a few feet, and took off at a run, straight into the air. She cannonballed into the lake with an ostentatious splash.

Her body sank into the cool water. She felt the heat of Vegas, the sweat of learning about Archie, the travel funk, all of it, wash away in the cool water.

Her feet landed on the sandy bottom. It must be about six feet deep here, she estimated. Hope used her hands to stay submerged for a few seconds. She was weightless.

She'd done this before. She used to do it all the time. She also used to do somersaults in the water, over and over. She couldn't even pinpoint the last time she went swimming.

Why had she stopped?

She saw Archie's eyes wandering to the younger women at the beach, the last time they tried to go on vacation.

She'd let his assessment of her beach body ruin her enjoyment of swimming. Or was that an excuse? Was she blaming him for her own self-doubt?

Whatever, she sluiced off thoughts of Archie like the water sluiced off her skin.

Hope kicked off the bottom and turned a somersault in the water.

There was no gravity. She could imagine herself as a gymnast or superhero. She could bend the air.

At one point, five somersaults in a row was her record. The tipsy feeling in her head kept her at one this time.

She swam to the surface. She turned over and floated, her face in the sunlight, her body floating on the surface.

It was a gorgeous feeling, swimming before lunch. Not worrying about her stupid stretch marks. She reached out her arms behind her and did a backstroke to swim out farther. Her shoulders released something, tension. Anger?

She concentrated on the strokes, on stretching her arms behind her. She was as fluid as she could be. She moved her body with intention. It was rusty, this motion. But it was still there. Her muscles and tendons remembered what to do. Her body was older, but her heart, it knew the beat, her breath, found a rhythm with her arms and legs. A rhythm she'd forgotten about but was always there, at the lake, in the water.

Hope paused and put her body upright in the lake. She turned to face the cottage.

She treaded water for a moment so she could see the little cottage from her new vantage point.

It was so cute. The windows on the lakeside were trimmed in

white. There was a little porch where she could envision a table and chairs. She spied an old-fashioned red kettle-style charcoal grill. Her mind went instantly to what she could make on it. Maybe as a thank you to Libby, she'd make her friend dinner.

And then the idea struck her. She was going fishing right now.

"I hope I didn't traumatize you too much with my backstroke, fishies, but it's about to get worse."

Hope kicked her legs. She sliced through the water with her favorite crawl stroke. Her arms were strong, thanks to her work in the kitchen.

She hoisted herself out of the water, grabbed her towel, and set out to find what she needed.

It wasn't thirty minutes later that she had a rod in hand and fishing line in Lake Manitou.

It was the one thing she and her dad had in common, fishing. It made her a little sad to think that he wasn't here anymore. While her relationship with her mother was fraught, her dad's main crime was passivity.

None of it mattered now. He'd left her with a love of fishing, something she hadn't done in ages and ages. And darn it if she wasn't going to catch something and make something special for Libby and J.J.

It was an all-afternoon affair, but in the end, she wound up with five blue gill and a yellow perch. She knew she'd be sunburned, but it didn't matter. She knew there were largemouth bass to be had, crappie probably too, but she didn't snare any of those beauties. But maybe tomorrow?

She'd spent the day fishing with no other care in the world. How had she not ever taken her own girls fishing?

She could blame Archie—he didn't like it—but it was her own fault. She should have taught them how to bait a hook, how to be patient, and how to recognize the local fish. She'd done none of it. There was more than just Archie to blame when it came to her regrets.

"I bet you regret swimming here, little fishes." Hope smiled as she gathered her bucket of fish.

She found a Styrofoam cooler in the little shed next to the cottage where she'd located the fishing gear. She deposited her catch, and all regrets of how she could have done better as a mother, or wife, were replaced for the moment with ideas on how best to cook this for dinner.

Hope showered off and hung her makeshift bathing suit, bra and underwear, on an old clothesline strung between two trees in the back. She was certain hundreds of beach towels and swimsuits had air dried over the years in this very spot.

She'd have to make a run to the grocery store if she was going to create the dish she wanted for Libby and J.J.

Did she remember how to get to town?

Hope hadn't looked at her phone or checked her messages or any of it. But she picked it up now to enter the grocery store into her GPS. She thought she'd seen it when they were downtown in Irish Hills yesterday. Barton's Food Village, that's what it was called back in the day.

Hope saw she'd missed a call: It was from her bank.

She hit redial.

"This is Marcia H. Venerable. I received a message to call back."

"Please hold."

After a minute of The Carpenters' easy listening hold music, a woman came on the line. "Ms. Venerable, can you provide the answer to your security question?"

Hope did as they asked.

"Thank you, Ms. Venerable. We had an interesting encounter earlier today. Your husband came into the branch and attempted to withdraw a significant amount of money."

"How significant?"

"Fifty thousand dollars."

Hope nearly choked.

"Does he *have* fifty thousand dollars?" Hope knew the joint account that they shared sure didn't have that sum.

"Um, no, he was trying to withdraw it from your business account."

"*Excuse* me?"

Hope had an account for her catering and contest win money. She'd always kept it separate, so she could keep her expenses in line. She used that account to buy supplies and ingredients and pay for travel to food competitions. Archie told her in no uncertain terms that he wouldn't pay for any of her cooking hobbies. She did it on her own. And had the meticulous accounting to prove where every dime went.

Her heart sank. She did have fifty thousand dollars. In fact, she had double that. Had her husband managed to steal her food contest winnings? She was at once terrified that he'd pilfered her hard-earned money, her business nest egg, and also infuriated. How low could he go?

"Well, he wasn't happy, but we had to let him know that you've not authorized anyone but yourself to access that account. If you need to add him, we can do that. We'd need to get your signature and his if you need him to have access—"

"—No, you're exactly right. Do not, I repeat, *do not* let him or anyone else touch those funds!"

A wave of relief swept over her. The money she'd earned with every spare moment of her time—learning, perfecting, resetting after losing, and trying again—was there. It was the most she'd ever had. And thanks to Archie telling her he wanted no part of her "hobby," it was protected from him.

Archie had tried to take her money. He'd slept with Bambi Carla, or whatever her name was, and now, knowing she'd just won the big prize, tried to take it!

"Glad we could help. In the future, if you do want to add someone, we're happy to do that as well."

"Nope, we're good as is. Thanks again."

She ended the call. She wanted to call Archie and yell and scream and vent. She ran her hand through her hair. That gray lock felt like it was getting wider as she thought about what Archie had done. Sleeping with the new receptionist at the dealership was one thing but taking her money was a new level.

Ha, they were supposed to be a team. She would have used that money for him or for them. She always did.

If he would have asked her for something, presented a bill that they needed to get paid, or given her the respect of congratulating her on earning over one hundred thousand for that account, she would have considered it theirs, not hers.

But the way he'd tried to do it behind her back made her think of it as hers, not his or even theirs.

Another separation happened at that moment. Hope got further away from Marcia H. Venerable and closer to Hope Benton.

Hope Benton had an idea, a dream, and it was getting more real with every second she spent here.

Just then, there was a knock at the screen door. Libby and J.J.

"Girl, your drawers are out on the line. I feel like you're my mom," J.J said.

Hope opened the screen door, and her two friends filled the little space.

"We came to kidnap you for dinner," Libby explained.

"Oh, sure, yes." Hope realized she was shaking.

"Honey, what's wrong?" J.J. put a hand on Hope's shoulder.

"I, uh, well, I knew my husband was low, but he sunk to a level below the basement today."

"I'm sorry, do you want to talk about it? Can we help? I know a voodoo priestess in Jackson. We could go the curse route?"

Hope laughed at the idea of an Archie doll being poked with needles. "No, actually, I think I've got a better idea. What do you say to a seasonal, all local summer dining experience in downtown Irish Hills?"

"Yes! I say yes!!" Libby said and clapped her hands.

"We were about to muscle you into it. Thank goodness we don't have to resort to violence," said J.J.

"No, I'm doing it. I want to do it. My dream has always been to open a restaurant, and you walked in like a fairy godmother and handed it to me."

"To be fair, we're the same age. I'm more like your fairy god girlfriend."

"Right, right, well, I'm in. One hundred percent."

J.J. and Libby circled Hope in a hug.

She was doing it. She wasn't going back to Archie. She was staying right here and figuring out how to find her own dreams. Without the girls, without her husband, and without her parents to tell her they were impossible.

"Okay, well, is now the time to talk about your underwear out there? It's way too old lady for you. Heck, I think Aunt Emma's are hotter than what's on that line," J.J. remarked.

Libby shook her head at J.J.'s assessment of Aunt Emma's underwear.

"Yeah, I used to buy bras that I thought were sexy. Now I buy them based on the criteria that they don't stab me to death, that's it," Hope said.

"Gotcha, honey, I think you've got a lot to fill us in on from your day," J.J. said.

"I do, but first, how about a run to the grocery store? I want to start experimenting with the fish I caught, and I ugh, well, I probably do need a proper bathing suit."

"Food Village it is, but stick to food, not fashion from there. I'll lend you a suit," Libby said.

"And I can provision us for summer water for the night," J.J. said.

"What?"

"Summer water is like regular water but with a daiquiri in it," J.J. explained.

"Daquiri, grilled fish, and borrowed swimsuit, if that's not a good night, I'm not sure what is," Hope said.

They piled into Libby's Jeep and headed downtown. Hope was giddy. She was going to do it. She was going to take this opportunity and give it everything she could. This time, finally, she was going for it. Archie had helped her see, even though she was sure that wasn't his intention. She needed to live for herself for once. If she didn't make her dream come true now, another decade could go by in a blink of an eye. That's one thing she knew for sure now that she was in her fifties: Time was fleeting, and opportunities like this were as rare as the connection she shared with Libby and Hope.

She had a lot to think about, but before anything else, she needed to make a fast change.

"Oh, Libby, I need a bank. Is there one that you recommend, for the restaurant and all that?"

"Sure, no problem. First National Bank has a branch in Onsted, but it's not that far of a drive. And there's a money machine in the grocery store. Which is nice, no fee to use if you're a First National customer."

"Great, thanks."

They headed into town.

Hope's marriage might be in a steaming pile of wreckage, but her finances didn't have to be. She would remove all her funds from the bank she currently shared with Archie. There would be no chance he could take what she'd worked for.

He was the past. Irish Hills and her own restaurant were the future.

She was taking bold steps. It felt right, even though it made her stomach feel a bit like it did when she did somersaults in the water.

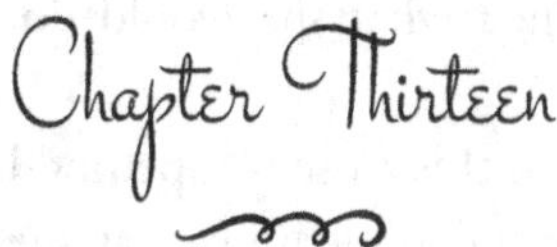

Chapter Thirteen

Hope

It wasn't the first time she'd thought about opening a restaurant. It wasn't the second time.

She'd thought about it over and over again from the time she was eighteen. Her dream glowed brightly at some points of her life and was barely an ember at other times.

But it was always there.

And it had started in Irish Hills with her grandmother. Grandma Benton encouraged her to dig in the dirt, pluck a tomato from the vine, and eat it with a sprinkle of salt. She learned if a fruit or vegetable was at its peak, there was no need to get fussy about how to serve it.

That was her foundation. That was the place she started with food.

Every meal she made, every recipe she invented, every cookbook she read, every morsel she ate, they were all filed away in her brain. Waiting for something. Maybe waiting for today.

She had honed her ideas, abandoned them, and then got them out again.

Now, finally, she could act.

Some people imagine what they would do if they won the lottery. Hope imagined what she would do if she had her own restaurant.

She'd never gotten this close to opening her own place. Here, in this moment, she felt confident in a way she never did at home.

The menu. The staff. The style. She was sure about it. She had a vision, a story to tell, and an experience she wanted to create for diners.

She wanted them to know the simple joy of eating foods grown right here, with recipes created to show them off.

Over the next few days, J.J. and Libby helped her with logistics and any questions she had.

Along with the perfect plates of food, Hope wanted people to feel joy at her table. She wanted to create for her guests, an atmosphere. She wanted the shared experience to glow in the memory of the diners, long after the meal was served.

As a practical matter, she decided she'd focus on dinner and lunch. Breakfast could come later if they succeeded.

Nothing about her restaurant would be fussy. Irish Hills wasn't a fussy place. The summer people were here to enjoy summer at the lake. Elevated dishes, for certain, that was her goal, but pretentious, never.

And summer would be the entire ballgame. If she was going to make seasonal food in Michigan work, it could only be open in the season.

The weather and the peak ripeness times for the ingredients she wanted to feature told her that she could only be open from Memorial Day to Halloween. Five months of the year. That was it. The other seven months, well, she wasn't sure about that. Maybe she'd cater back in Covington. Maybe in Michigan?

Hope didn't want to overthink that. She worried her five

month concept, would mean Libby would rescind the offer. Maybe Libby needed something there year-round, something more traditional? But when she explained it, Libby didn't push, and Hope was grateful.

Five months of all out work. Five months during the ripeness of Michigan. Five months to give her everything to the restaurant.

If she could launch the restaurant her way, she'd improvise the rest. Without the responsibility of mothering her girls or being the backstop to Archie's life, she would give herself the freedom to learn, to experiment.

And the menu for the restaurant started to form in her mind. She could see her customers. She could see what they had on their plates.

It had been two days since she'd committed to opening a restaurant. It had been a whirlwind two days.

She started each day with a morning swim. It was bracing this early in June, but it cleared her head. It sharpened her focus and gave her the zing she needed to work late into the night on the restaurant.

She took her swim, got dressed, and drove her borrowed old pickup to the restaurant. Libby had given her the keys to the building, and most mornings, Dean's crews were arriving when she did. The sound of people working on the adjacent buildings filled her with energy. There was something exciting about to happen here.

She didn't have furniture yet—of course, that was on her list of things to do—so she was sitting on a folding chair in the center of the empty restaurant space, looking at the list she'd taken to keeping on yellow notepads, when a little old lady walked in.

She probably wanted breakfast. It had happened twice already, people thinking they could come on in and have a meal when they saw the lights were now on inside.

"I'm sorry, ma'am. We're not open yet."

"I know, Hope, I know. But I had to get my eyes on your face."

"Oh, my gosh! Aunt Emma!"

Emma was Libby's aunt, but they all claimed her.

Hope stood up, and the two embraced. She was so little, this woman, but a force of nature and a giant in Hope's memory.

"You grew into a beautiful woman, as I knew you would. You and Libby with those long legs."

"Oh, I don't know. I've pretty much given up on worrying about beauty. But thank you."

"Nonsense, you're in the prime of your life!"

Hope smiled and speculated at how old Aunt Emma must be to make that statement.

"Well, if I live to be one hundred."

"I'm on my way, and I couldn't be happier. And good for you; you're right to keep that lock of gray. It's striking."

Aunt Emma's hair was snow-white. It had been ever since Hope could remember. She was a silver sister before it was a fad.

"My dear niece said you had questions about connecting to some local vendors for this restaurant. What's the place going to be called?"

"Not sure yet. My catering business was Venerable Catering, maybe something like that. I'm still noodling that one."

"Hmm." Aunt Emma wiggled her head back and forth as though she wasn't quite sold on that name.

Hope forged ahead. "I'm looking for locally sourced, sustainable, in-season food."

"Locally sourced, sustainable in-season food was just called food, in my day. All these words. You need farmers. That's what you need. Like your grandparents, I sure do miss the Bentons."

It was sweet to hear someone remember her grandparents, who'd been gone for decades now.

Hope was excited about the local produce, but the local protein was another issue entirely. She had no idea about where that would come from.

"Are there any commercial fishermen around here?"

"That's tougher. Not sure about fish. But I'll give you all the names I have. I can connect you with half a dozen farmers, two dairy outfits that do milks and cheese, and a pig farm. That's Dean Tucker's cousin who's got the pig farm. Also, a hooch farm or two."

"Hooch farm?"

"Winery in Lenawee County and a Distillery in Clinton, just east on Route Twelve.

"Perfect. I can't thank you enough. This will eliminate hours and hours of leg work."

Aunt Emma smiled and looked at her, really looked at her. "The five of you girls were something else. The Sandbar Sisters. You've taken care of your husband and children. It's time you put yourself first, this dream first. You know, our dreams don't come true without a little muscle to make them happen. Do you understand?"

Hope felt a catch in her throat. No one talked to her that way. The old woman was telling her to be who she wanted to be, not a version of what others thought she should be.

"I do, finally. And it appears they also need a push from you and Libby."

"Well, yes, we're pushy, but in a good way." Aunt Emma smiled.

"I'm sorry I never came back. I mean, the last time I saw anyone was in '89. Not only did we have the tornado damage, but there was that Bruce guy. We all thought we were going straight to hell for not letting him in Nora House during the tornado."

"Oh, that, yes, a bit of a miscommunication there."

Hope narrowed her eyes at the older woman. "Hmm, yes, I heard. It seems that was a bit more than miscommunication."

"He's fine, or was, then. Who knows now? What I do know is guilt is a waste of time. I kick myself anytime I think any of you girls tortured yourselves over that deadbeat. I haven't."

"Well, I don't know about torture. I had other things happening, too, back at home. Being a young mom put the brakes on summers off."

"I imagine so. How old's that oldest daughter of yours?"

"Almost thirty-two."

Aunt Emma gave her a smile. She knew. She understood. Neither J.J. nor Libby had pressed her too much. They knew Archie was cheating. They knew her life had just blown up in the last few days.

They didn't know how her life really blew up right after she left Lake Manitou forever.

* * *

Hope, 1990

Eleven weeks ago, she'd snuck out to hang out with Archie to spite her mother.

The worst thing she could think of was being forced to go to University of Cincinnati and get a degree in accounting or hospital administration or whatever else her parents insisted was a safe choice with good job opportunities.

What she wouldn't give for that to be her problem now.

Her problem now was not throwing up as she walked down the aisle.

Archie, the cool guy with a cool car, was now reluctantly at the other end of the aisle. He did look handsome, Hope thought, in his rented tuxedo.

Archie's stupid friends, though, they had snuck beer into the church. They were good and buzzed already and laughing as Hope made her way to the end of the aisle.

She glanced at her mother. Stiff, erect posture, her lips grimacing. There was no sentimental moment before Hope's walk. Her mother was not a sentimental woman, and she was as mad about this as she was about everything else in life.

Archie took her arm; he was being sweet. He'd actually handled all this well. From the moment she found out she was pregnant; he'd been pretty decent about it all.

His reaction gave her some hope. Maybe this would all be okay.

Though, her dreams of any sort of education were now totally smashed to pieces. Her mother and father said they'd pay for a wedding. That was it. School? How was she going to do that while pregnant?

Because pregnant she was. Morning sickness pregnant. Bright pink line on the stick pregnant. Rabbit deader than hell pregnant.

It wasn't like the movie *Father of the Bride*, not one bit like that.

The mother of the bride was livid, the father of the bride was writing checks, while the bride herself was shell-shocked. For his part, the groom was doing his best. Hope did see that.

Don't get sick at the altar. Worse yet, don't get sick on *the altar.* That was her mantra on the big day. She was nauseated most of the time, and it erupted everywhere. It would be a scene more like *The Exorcist* if she was the barfing bride.

Leading up to her special day, Hope had thrown up in the waste can at the courthouse when they got their license, she'd ralphed out the window of Archie's Camaro on the way to sign the lease on the apartment, and an hour before the actual ceremony, she'd heaved into a garment bag as she removed her hot rollers. Luckily, her wedding dress wasn't still in the garment bag at the time.

Archie's cousin Paul "The Situation" Manos was a DJ on the weekends, so they'd got him on a discount. Archie's big Greek family was sweet and loving, the opposite of hers. They'd helped her smile multiple times during this weird, life-changing event she'd found herself in.

True, her mother had stepped up when it came to hastily pulling together a complete wedding and reception with the requisite bells and whistles. Her mother was efficient. She had booked the church, the hall, the food, all in a few short weeks.

Her instructions were concise, and her decisions rapid and definitive. It would be amazing to watch if it wasn't for the fact that her mother had decided her entire future without asking Hope what she thought of anything. Hope wasn't even allowed to hate pink for the bridesmaids. It was pink, like it or not.

"Make sure there's a bucket behind the altar," her mother told the church lady, who also doubled as the organist.

"Mom, jeez," she said, trying to assert herself. She knew full well this was all happening because she was pregnant, but still, it was supposed to be her big day. No matter how they got there.

Sharon Benton would not be chastised, though. "What? Just make sure it's a pink bucket, so it matches the bridesmaid dresses," Sharon amended the instruction with a little dig at her daughter.

Hope sighed. *Here comes the bride.*

Hope and Archie said, "I do." And mercifully, Hope's prayer was answered. She didn't puke while at the altar.

Instead, she had to run like an Olympic sprinter during "The Chicken Dance" and lost it behind the bar.

It was a very special moment, on her very special day.

Chapter Fourteen

Hope, Present Day

Hope hadn't talked about her shotgun wedding in quite a while. It was a thing, back then, getting married before she started to "show."

Funny how much has changed in the three decades since. If either of her girls were in the same boat, she would never in a million years expect them to marry if that's not what they wanted. Or to quit school.

Aunt Emma was a good listener. And somehow, Hope felt lighter telling her about that time in her life. She would eventually share it with the Sandbar Sisters, she knew. They all had decades of adventures and misadventures to share.

Telling Aunt Emma why, among other reasons, she never returned to Irish Hills was enough for now.

"You had your hands full, very young."

"I did, that's true. It all worked out, though. My girls are amazing. If they'd ever call me back."

Hope had left a message, albeit a strange rambling one, with both the girls. About separating from their dad and opening a restaurant. No calls back as of yet, though.

"Oh, they will. Don't worry about that. And don't worry about homicide by tornado. He was alive and kicking when I kicked him out of town."

"Good, thank you. I did have nightmares early on, but then I had other tornadoes, so to speak, to deal with."

"No worrying about the past, not when we have so much to do to face the amazing future!"

"True. So, your list of possible vendors?"

"Hand me your notepad."

Hope did as instructed.

In pretty cursive, Aunt Emma wrote a list of farmers, the winery, and other locals Hope should check out.

"Here, every name on this list is a good source for your new venture."

"I'll call them all and pay a visit."

"Wonderful. I'd do it fast, though. July Fourth is less than a month away. Tick tick!"

"Yes, true."

Hope had no idea why the tick tick, but then Aunt Emma was old, and some of the stuff she said was probably nutty.

Tick tick?

"Okay, well, that's taken care of. I've got several more errands to get to. Tonight is movie night, and I may be in good health, but if I don't take a little beauty nap beforehand, I fall right asleep. It drives Peter to distraction."

"Peter?

"My lawyer, he's waiting in the car. Let me know if you have any trouble with those farmers or other names on that list. Trust me, they all owe me a favor."

"And now I do too."

"Oh, I'm sure I'll collect, in a free dinner, very soon!"

She helped Aunt Emma to the door and saw the waiting car, with Peter, the attorney chauffeur, waiting in the driver's seat.

"And whatever you do, please, no paper placemats in this place. Keep it classy."

"Will do."

Aunt Emma left for her beauty rest, and Hope looked at the list. Time to start making relationships with the vendors and farmers if she was going to pull off her local menu concept.

Her plan was going to be different from any restaurant in the area. She knew this. And she knew it would be challenging to do.

Hope sifted through the pages of her rapidly filling yellow notepads.

If she wanted everything on the menu sourced from the area, could she also fill this space with local ceramics, artwork, and linens? She knew it would be more work to go this route, but it was central to her idea of her dream restaurant.

She thought back to her grandparents' farm, which was small compared to some in the area. She remembered picking peaches at Kapnick's Orchard and getting sour cherries at Hide Away farms.

Her grandpa had let all five of her friends roam around the edge of the farm, picking strawberries he planted.

She could still taste the strawberry shortcake concoction she'd invented in Aunt Emma's kitchen. Libby was not into baking, and neither was Goldie. But J.J. and Viv were her willing sous chefs back then. Before they knew that was a job.

She envisioned her changing menu. She'd create dishes that took advantage of fresh asparagus in spring and fat blackberries in July.

Hope looked at the list from Aunt Emma. What was the top priority? It was a bit daunting, considering she didn't have one thing accomplished yet.

Libby and J.J. had offered to help but Hope knew they were also busy. J.J. was a hairstylist, and Libby ran the world, as far as Hope could see.

First thing's first. She needed equipment and staff. That could take the longest to get in place. So, she started there.

The restaurant already had a dishwasher and a mixer. It needed a range and oven immediately. Hope had cash, thanks to her win, so she could invest in some of the things they'd need. She probably should have come to some agreement with Libby about who owned what in here. She made a note to talk it over with her old friend. She wanted this to work, but also, what if she couldn't pull this off? If someone else took over this space, Libby would need to know what Hope had purchased. Friendships ended over money misunderstandings. Hope wasn't going to let that happen, not after just finding Libby and J.J. again.

Hope ripped a sheet of paper from her notebook and wrote, Help Wanted, in big block letters with a black Sharpie. She added her cellphone number and taped it to the window. She locked up, and then she went out to the truck. She'd probably have to put the job openings online somewhere, but at least if there was someone local looking for a job, she had a sign up.

She had the afternoon. She was going to check in on Aunt Emma's list. Sure, she could call, but what she wanted was to build relationships. To figure out how to work with the growers to create from what they had.

Behind the wheel of the pickup truck, windows open, Hope traveled up and down the country roads that provided a patchwork between the lakes.

She made deals with two local vegetable farmers. She arranged for them to bring the produce to her when they could. If they couldn't, she made a note of that too. She'd be driving a lot and picking up a lot if she didn't get a staff together. She wondered if Libby would sell her this truck.

She knew Libby was being generous to get Hope to stay and open the restaurant. But she did have her winnings and some extra from her catering business. If this succeeded, she'd need to pay her way. But she wasn't stupid. If this failed, she didn't want to be destitute. Her freedom from Archie right now was dependent on her taking the right steps and letting Libby be generous for now.

It was a productive afternoon; she'd sourced a few things on her list.

But she still needed staff. She'd need a sous chef, three servers, a busboy, and a dishwasher at least.

She jotted more things down on her notepad and flipped to the next page. Hope thought of four more things to add.

"I'll never be done if I keep adding to the list."

She was back at the little cottage that evening with a new list and her phone.

She drank a glass of wine from Cherry Creek, thanks to Aunt Emma, and a listing online caught her eye.

It was a used but workable commercial-grade oven with eight gas burners and was local. That could be something! She messaged the seller.

She needed to get moving. She had evening plans with Libby and J.J.

Her phone buzzed, and she looked at the caller ID.

It was Julia, her oldest. Finally.

"What the heck is happening? Dad says you've lost your mind and essentially run away from home."

"Hello, Julia."

"Mom, hello, but what?"

It was one thing sharing the sordid collapse of your marriage with your old friends. It was something else telling your kids that their dad was cheating on their mom.

Hope struggled for the right words. Her girls weren't girls anymore. They were adults. But still, the instinct to protect them, to shield them from pain, was as strong now as it was when they were toddlers.

"Your dad is in a relationship with someone else, I found out." She stopped. She let that sink in. She did her best to squelch the desire to want her daughters to take sides.

"Are you sure? I mean, really?"

"Yes, your dad isn't too clear on how Apple photo clouds work." That was all she should say. It was too much. She wouldn't want to have heard it about her own father. But there it was.

The line was quiet.

"Oh, gross. I'm sorry I asked. Ugh, so you're in Wisconsin or something?"

"Michigan, Irish Hills. I spent summers here growing up. An old friend offered me a place to stay on Lake Manitou. It's really charming; you should—"

"—Mom, vacation? Your marriage is falling apart, and you're on vacation?"

"I'm not on vacation. That's the thing I wanted to tell you. I'm opening a restaurant. Right here. It's going to be amazing. I mean, there's so much to do, and I have no idea where I'm going to source everything, but still, it's my—"

"Mom, I can't process all this right now. I'm sorry about Dad, I am. But you can't mean you're staying there and just letting Dad stay in Covington. That you can't work something out? I mean, don't all men Dad's age have midlife crisis issues? It could pass. This can all work out."

Hope didn't want to break Julia's heart, but it was time she stopped living for her kids or in fear of Archie's judgment. She wasn't going to lie to spare her children. They weren't children.

"The thing is, Julia, I think I want to be here, Dad or not. Things are working out for me."

"Who *are* you? This is *bananas*."

"Listen, I'm going to text you the address. If you get some time and want to do a weekend, or week or whatever, you could come visit."

"And Dad?"

Hope didn't tell her daughter about the second betrayal she'd experienced, Archie trying to grab her prize money. It was enough that her daughter understood that Hope was moving on.

"I wish him, uh, I wish him well. But my life is unfolding here, right now, without him."

"And us, me, and Sara?"

"I love you both. You're welcome to be here with me whenever you want. That won't change. I want to build something you'll be proud of, but more than that, something I'll be proud of."

"Have you been reading *Untamed* again?" her daughter asked.

"Ha, no, currently Brené Brown."

"Ugh, Mom, I'm not taking care of Dad."

"He's a grown man. He'll be just fine."

"Okay...well, I love you."

"Love you too, honey."

They ended the call. Hope felt a little lighter. Her daughter would be okay. It was strange to think of your parents as people with lives, dreams, and disappointments. And for so long, she'd done all she could to ensure her kids had the lives they deserved.

She'd given that to them. Now it was time to give it to herself.

Chapter Fifteen

Hope

She'd put together a salad from fresh lettuce she'd bought from the farms she'd visited, added a goat cheese she'd found from a local vendor, and whipped up her shallot vinaigrette to take to Libby's this evening.

She was looking forward to hanging out with the girls. Hope had mom friends. She had clients. She even had food competition buddies. But she didn't have a group like this. Friends who remembered who she was, her history, and who, after all this time, clicked back into place like no time had gone by. Maybe that was the gift of her midlife, time to simply be with people she loved, even more than the chance at the restaurant.

Hope pulled the top knot she'd been sporting all day and ran her fingers through her hair at her scalp. The hair hurt, if that was possible, from being bound up all day. She looked in the mirror and added a little mascara and lip gloss.

Not too terrible for fifty, she thought.

She liked her white streak, was grateful for the thick hair she used to try to thin with flat irons, and there were wrinkles, to be sure, but she was getting used to them.

Hope opened the screen door to leave, and a flurry of feathers and screeching burst in through the door and into the cottage.

Hope Venerable prided herself on keeping an even keel. She was a full-grown, not hysterical adult. But as it registered in her brain that two birds had burst into the cottage and were frantically batting their wings against each other and every surface of the place, she screamed. The birds also screamed or screeched or whatever birds do.

Her heart felt like it might explode with the sudden shock of the melee. She needed a tennis racket or a net or something.

Hope flapped her arms. "Go, shoo, get out of here!"

The windows all had screens. There was no way to usher the birds that way. They needed to go out the way they came in. Through the door.

"Here! Here!!" She yelled at them as though they spoke English.

"Miss, are you okay in there?" a male voice called into the cottage.

She didn't have time for that. What? Was she okay? "No!"

The screen door opened, and a shirtless man in faded jeans appeared. He slammed the screen door open, bursting in almost as dramatically as the birds had entered.

She saw he had a sidearm on his belt. She saw taught muscle and sinew coiled for action.

What was happening? Was she being robbed?

"Holy crap!"

He must have seen her eyes bug at the site of the firearm.

"I'm a police officer. Are you in danger?"

"No, um, unless they have the bird flu. Ahhh!"

The two birds swooped from the ceiling and grazed her head. She swatted them and turned in a circle.

"I need to get them out of here."

"Hang on!"

The shirtless stranger ran out the same way he came in. Hope watched the birds careen around, squawk, and panic, realizing they were trapped—worse, trapped together!

The shirtless stranger walked in again. This time he had her fishing net.

"Stand back. I don't want to accidentally hit you." He was used to giving orders and having them followed.

Hope did as instructed. She certainly didn't know how to get rid of wildlife going bonkers in an enclosed space. In fact, she'd forgotten the net was out on the porch. She backed up, and the man used it to herd the tumble of birds back toward the door. Hope raced over and opened the screen.

"It's working! Go on, get out of here," she said.

Hope tried not to notice that the man, while gray-haired, was rather ripped. *I mean*, she thought, *he's shirtless. What else am I supposed to do but notice his abs?*

He followed the birds with the net, and somehow, he got them to the door. He followed behind them as they flapped their way through door and back outside.

Hope brought up the tail end of the strange melee and closed the screen door behind her. The avian war proceeded out into the trees. And Hope tried to find her composure, which she'd completely lost a second ago. Not exactly how she liked to present herself upon meeting new people, especially new people with guns and, uh, guns.

"Thank you."

"I thought someone was being murdered in here."

"I, uh, yeah, I screamed. They squawked; they brought a pitched battle into my kitchen. It totally startled me. In fact, maybe get the paddles. I thought I had a heart attack for a second."

"Really? I can call nine-one-one for help if you think you're in distress." His eyes turned from intense to gentle, and they were blue, really blue, she noticed.

"No, I'm kidding. I'm Hope and fine."

"I hope you're fine too."

"No, my name, it's Hope."

"Ah, I'm Greg McQueen."

"Nice to meet you. So, the uniform, this is standard issue for Irish Hills?"

"Ha, yeah, this is embarrassing. I'm next door. Just got home and heard the screaming."

"Ah."

"There's my place, see, one dock over. Welcome, sorry about our rude avian population. Though, I don't think they were fighting if you know what I mean."

"Uh, um, oh." Hope realized what he meant. She hoped she wasn't blushing; she was way too old for that! If her face was red, though, maybe Greg McQueen would think she'd had a cardiac episode. Somehow that was preferable.

"Well, aggressively amorous birds, armed strangers, it's supposed to be a quiet little spot."

"It normally is. I haven't had a neighbor in a long time. I guess I'm out of practice."

"Yeah, standard neighbor greetings are more along the lines of borrowing a cup of sugar, maybe?"

"You were screaming loudly."

Hope was totally embarrassed now that she'd lost her cool like a cartoon housewife encountering a mouse.

"I didn't know anyone was around, much less a half-naked-gun-toting, ugh, neighbor."

Greg McQueen laughed at her description. "True, true, I mean, next time you're in trouble and need my help, I'll be sure to grab a shirt and a formal introduction request from Emma Francis Quinn."

"Good, yes, that seems appropriate," Hope laughed.

"Now, I'm going to go home unless there are other woodland creatures that I can help you dispatch?"

"No. I'm good. It looks like the love birds are gone."

"Nice to meet you, Hope," Greg McQueen flashed a handsome smile at her. Oh, this one was trouble, and he knew it! Hope decided his jawline could cut glass and break hearts. For a moment she remembered the old Hope, the one that used to shamelessly flirt as a pastime. She stifled the urge, that was a younger version of her. This version of Hope had had wrinkles, gray hair, and probably seemed totally inept to the next door neighbor man.

"Thank you for the assistance. And I'm sorry I made you think there was an ax murderer in here."

"You're welcome, and I mean, I didn't think you were someone who worried about formal attire. I mean, you do swim in your underwear, so." Whoa! Greg McQueen beat her to the flirt.

Her new neighbor gave her a wink and walked swiftly toward his cottage.

Oh, my goodness, he'd seen her in her underwear in the water! She'd thought she was alone. In an effort to defend herself, she called after him, "I didn't know anyone was around!"

"Didn't say I minded," Greg McQueen replied as he disappeared into the neighboring cottage.

Well, that was some first impression she'd made.

* * *

A few minutes later, Hope stood, salad in hand and pride in the dustbin, waiting for her ride. The girls picked her up on the water, not on the road.

Hope didn't look back to the neighboring cottage again, fearing she'd say or do something ridiculous. Swimming in her skivvies and screaming bloody murder at a pair of amorous robins were enough for one week.

A red and silver vessel came into view soon after her encounter, thank goodness! She could flee.

At the helm of the slow-moving but glorious old boat was another old friend she hadn't seen forever and ever.

"Captain Keith."

Keith was the honorary sixth Sandbar Sister. He was like a brother to all of them—well, all of them except, of course, Libby. It had been obvious to everyone but them that he was in love with Libby all those summers ago.

"Hiya, it's been a while," Keith said.

They docked the boat.

"Permission to come aboard," Hope asked Keith.

"Oh, it's her boat. I'm just the hired help."

"Permission granted," Libby said.

Keith put his arms out. Hope stepped inside and couldn't really believe this middle-aged man was Keith. He was still handsome and boyish at the same time. But the gawkiness of youth was a memory. He was a vet, had lost his wife, Libby had told her. He had been through so much.

She thought back to the time Keith took the hit for things they asked him to do, from running off boys they didn't want to waste time on, to telling ones they did that they were interested.

The stuff he'd put up with from them! Suddenly, she was flooded with love for him, for J.J. and Libby.

"Wow, this is weird," she said.

"Weird and totally normal at the same time," J.J. pointed out. She was right.

Libby and Keith had rekindled their relationship after all these years. It made Hope so happy to see.

And also sad, that her life, since the time she knew them, had changed so drastically. Her personality as Mrs. Marcia Venerable was nothing like it had been when they knew her.

The Hope Benton they knew was in charge of her teenage love life. But that self-assured teen turned into a disappointed wife.

During her entire marriage with Archie she tried to find a way to make him feel as cool as he seemed when they first met. She was attracted to Archie because he made her mom mad. It wasn't the best foundation for a harmonious adult relationship.

She shook it off. And the melancholy that wanted to overcome her when she thought about time past, and time wasted.

"Find a comfortable spot on the floating porch, and I'll ferry you three ladies around the lake," Keith said.

"Like old times," Hope said.

"Yes, exactly, except no backseat boat driving." Keith pointed that statement at Libby.

She responded by swatting him on the hip.

They seemed easy together. It was sweet. Hope was glad J.J. was also solo on this little trip. It saved her from feeling like a fifth wheel with these two.

"What's been up with your life?" Hope asked Keith. "I can't believe how long it's been?"

"These days," he replied, "two of my sons run Steve's Marina with me."

"Wow, you bought the Marina, nice. Does it still have a restaurant?"

She remembered getting burgers on the water at Steve's Marina back in the day.

"It's there but not opened. We've got docking and repair and winter storage. Maybe someday we'll get the restaurant going if this one has her way."

Libby was always working to make plans, take charge, and clearly, she had a million plans for their old stomping grounds.

"Downtown first, let's meet that deadline," Libby said. It was almost like she was telling herself to hold her own horses.

"And then the world," J.J. announced.

Deadline? Hope meant to ask about that, she was aiming for the holiday week. But that was a goal, not a deadline.

This wasn't a work meeting. These were old friends, ancient friends, trying to bridge the gap of decades. And doing it pretty well. Hope was glad to see. They were comfortable with each other, even though so much time had passed.

She turned to J.J. Her friend was so totally herself; she hated the phrase spunky, but, well, J.J. was, then and now.

"Where's Dean tonight?" she asked her.

"Working. He's traveling to Flat Rock and said he needs to get some wiring stuff, so we're all set for the inspections next week."

"I hadn't even asked about all that," Hope confessed.

"You worry about health department inspections. I'll worry about building ones," Libby said.

Keith took them slowly around the lake. They'd set up the food in the center of the boat. J.J. generously filled her glass with wine.

The sun had burned bright yellow all day, but now as it set, it mellowed into a beautiful gold. The light turned everything the same color as the white wine they were sipping.

She caught up with J.J's life story as best she could. From her work at the salon to marrying Dean and becoming a mom to catching Hope up on J.J.'s mom.

J.J. told Hope that her mom was living in Florida but on the way back for the summer.

"Michigan, beware. Jacqueline Pawlak is headed back. We stock up on cigs, red licorice, and patience when she's here. She also insists I pull her hair through a cap. She's the only one who I still do that for, but no other way will do for mom's frosted highlights."

"Oh, and you remember J.J.'s brother Jared?" Libby added. "He's good to know these days. He owns the Peck's Hardware."

"Oh, that little pudding. Oh, wow, that sounds mean now. Did we scar him for life?" Hope said. That was their nickname for J.J.'s little brother.

"Still a pudding inside," J.J said.

"But buff on the outside. He's saved my bacon for the million repairs I needed to do at Nora House," Libby said.

The good wine and good company prompted Hope to share the good story of her scandalous meeting with the next-door neighbor.

"Well, just so you know, I'm likely to get arrested for indecency," Hope said.

"What, now you're talking," J.J. said.

"Yeah, I had no idea that I had a neighbor in the next door cottage."

"Oh, you met Greg. He's a good guy," Keith said.

"Well, I hope so. I mean, the man's seen me at my worst twice now. Day one, I didn't have a bathing suit, so I took a dip in my old granny panties."

"I'd say he's a lucky son of a gun. You're a hot mama," J.J. said.

"Yeah, well, not exactly how I envisioned meeting my new neighbors."

"Greg's actually retired from the Detroit Police Department. He's contracting with the Lenawee County Sheriff's Office here, as needed. Since Irish Hills is too little to have a police force. He's been great," Libby said.

"Not a creepy stalker?" Hope replied.

"Nah, well, not that I'm aware of." Libby shrugged.

But it was clear they liked her neighbor. Which made today's bird incident even more embarrassing.

"My formal introduction included me screaming bloody murder because a couple birds invaded the house, right before you guys picked me up, actually. I'm screaming, and this shirtless man with a sidearm shows up to rescue me from what I'm sure sounded like murderers, marauders, or pirates. I was screaming like it could have been all of the above."

"Shirtless, whoa, so a full view of all the guns, lucky you," J.J. said.

Libby rolled her eyes.

"You're a married woman, J.J. Tucker," Keith said.

"Yes, Dean's aware that I've got a dirty mind. It's one of my best qualities," J.J. said.

Hope's cheeks hurt from smiling and laughing with these three.

It had been a long time, and as Keith slowly rounded Lake Manitou for the third time, she was very glad that they decided to take a fourth loop.

Despite the invading birds and inadvertent exhibitionism, Hope was feeling like she was going in the right direction. For the first time in decades.

As they floated on the water, J.J. leaned toward her. "Here's what I've been wondering, you're a brilliant chef and always were. Why didn't you open a restaurant before now? What got in the way?"

"No one thing...everything. Just life."

Chapter Sixteen

Hope, 1995

Julia was watching *Gullah Gullah Island*. Hope thanked whoever was in charge of making TV shows for kids for *Gullah Gullah Island*. She couldn't take much more, *Barney*.

Sara was still taking an afternoon nap. She thanked the Lord for that afternoon nap. During the brief and rare lull that was life with toddlers, Hope ran out to the mailbox outside of their apartment.

Her stomach felt disconnected from her body. She'd checked the box obsessively this week. She opened the lid, and there was one thick envelope.

She pulled it out, and there was the Cincinnati State logo in the corner.

She slipped open the seal.

"Congratulations, and we're excited to welcome you...."

She was in! She'd applied to The Midwest Culinary Institute at Cincinnati State and had been holding her breath ever since. She was hopeful but worried. She'd done more diaper changing than recipe building in the last few years.

But they had accepted her application. It wasn't even far away! Cincinnati State was the best option for her life, and right now was the time. The girls were in preschool. They weren't infants anymore.

There was no way when she first got married, pregnant with Julia, and then pregnant again with Sara, that they could afford culinary school.

Archie and Hope struggled to pay for rent, diapers, formula, and all that came with having a young family. But it was getting easier as the girls got older.

She was able to save more and more of her tips.

Every day she spent at the restaurant was another day her career path galvanized. She wanted her career to be about food, to open her own place someday. Or invent a food product. Or be a caterer. She didn't have an exact plan for the next part, but she knew she needed to learn more.

That's where Cincinnati State came in.

Hope just needed to convince Archie. He was usually irritated when he came home. She knew selling cars was hard, that dealing with customers all day was tough, and that Archie's manager "never signs off" on the deals he tried to make.

Archie wasn't going to be an easy sell, but she had a plan. She rehearsed her pitch to Archie in her head. In the long run, getting this education would help them get ahead. Even if, in the short term, their budget would be even tighter. She had saved, so they had, at least, some of the money for this.

Hope worked all afternoon and into the evening to make things as peaceful as possible when Archie came home. She had the girls bathed and fed already, and she popped *The Little Mermaid* in the VHS player. They were happily "Under the Sea" when Archie walked in the door.

"Ugh, that one again, how many times? If I have to listen to it again, I'm going to break a dinglehopper off in someone's—"

"—Archie, come on, it keeps them quiet. Sit. I made you a steak and baked potato with the homemade sour cream you like."

Archie wasn't into her more creative attempts in the kitchen. He liked the basics. Hope was pulling out all the stops.

Archie took a seat at the little table in the middle of their apartment kitchen. There was only space for a table for two. The four of them couldn't all fit for the same meal.

"Wow, yeah, that looks amazing." Archie grabbed his knife and started slicing away at the steak she'd prepared for him.

"I thought you'd be hungry. I know it's been nuts at work."

"Hmm, yeah." Archie shoveled the food into his mouth, not waiting for her to sit or even checking to see if she was eating with him.

She brushed it off. She was used to him now, his quirks. He'd also been handed a lot of responsibility, just like her. She tried to remember that he'd never shirked it or tried to run away from their surprise family.

And in the end, surprise was the word. Her mother had called it an accident. That seemed wrong to her. An accident was a spill or something that needed to be cleaned up. She loved her girls; they weren't planned, but they were her joy.

A surprise, yes, accident, no.

"I have some news," Hope said.

Archie was scooping the sour cream onto the baked potato. His attention was focused on that, not her; hopefully, it was putting him in a good frame of mind.

"So, listen," Archie said, ignoring Hope's announcement that she had news.

"Okay, but then I have—"

Hope didn't have a chance to finish the sentence.

"—I put a down payment on a house in Covington."

"What?"

They had lived in this apartment since Julia was one. It was small but cute. She had a mom friend who lived three doors over. It was in a decent neighborhood. She didn't need to move, not now, when she wanted to spend what little extra money they had on tuition at Cincinnati State.

"Yeah, between us, we had the down payment. So, my manager, he's selling his ranch house in Covington. Really good schools, he said. It's not on the market yet. I had to move fast. Luckily, we had just enough."

"But that was both our money—"

"—Yeah, well, your part made a difference, for sure. Wait until you see it. Two-car garage, shed. It's near Taylor Mills Elementary. So, boom. You're welcome."

Hope smiled, but she felt hot tears in the back of her eyes. She blinked them away. She walked over to the sink. Her appetite for the meal she'd prepared was gone.

"I wish I could have seen it before you put the money down, and I mean, it is a joint account, and I was thinking maybe we had to talk about what to do with that."

"What's to talk about? Real estate is where it's at for our future. I mean, the dealership is okay, but we're going to buy this house, fix it up, and then sell it, and do it again and again. It's called flipping."

"Flipping?"

"Yeah, I signed up for a day-long class on how to do it. That wasn't cheap either, but it is an investment too."

"Oh."

Archie explained how they were going to become rich flipping houses. And yet...Hope had done every upgrade they'd made to their apartment by herself. She had hung the wallpaper, got approval from the landlord to paint, and she'd scrubbed the stove until the skin on her knuckles cracked so it would be clean and workable for them.

But somehow, Archie was going to flip houses?

"Don't you have to be good at home improvement stuff and do it fast to be profitable?"

"I'll figure it out. Rick, you remember him, he works in the service department. He just made thirty grand on a flip. This is the ticket."

"How much was it, the down payment?" Maybe it wasn't their whole nest egg?

"Ha, oh yeah, don't write a check. We're down to two hundred bucks in the checking."

The money they'd saved, it wasn't much. But it was a lot for them. And it was gone. Archie had decided what to spend it on.

Hope had worried herself sick about broaching the subject of spending money on her degree, and Archie hadn't thought twice about doing it without even telling her.

"Wow, so you put twelve thousand to the house. Okay." She knew her voice was wavering.

Archie caught it. He stood up and came over to her at the sink. He put his arms around her waist and buried his head in her neck. "Look, babe, I had to move fast. And this is just the beginning. We're going to turn this into a huge windfall."

"Okay."

He squeezed her tight.

He was right. The girls were getting bigger. They'd need to start kindergarten in a good school district. A house was a good investment. Archie had got the house for them. It was a family decision versus the one she'd made for herself.

Hope didn't even mention culinary school. She could wait.

She put the acceptance letter in the garbage, and for good measure, she scraped Archie's plate on top of it when she was doing the dishes.

Chapter Seventeen

Hope, Present Day

Hope saw the reply in her inbox. The commercial oven and range combo unit was still available!

Once she had that installed, she'd be ready to cook, test, and experiment with all her ideas for the menu.

She used her phone's GPS to navigate to the Irish Hills Country Club, despite the fact she'd worked at the club as a beer cart girl. It had been good for extra cash back in the day. But dodging passes from drunk golfers had been more challenging than dodging errant golf balls.

The smell of cut grass and the sound of the massive sprinklers shooting water into the fairways brought back memories of her time working here. She kept the windows rolled down as she made her way up the winding drive to the clubhouse.

She realized she had a smile on her face; both the memory of the past and the future of her business had put it there.

This was the last big piece of equipment she'd need for the

restaurant. Once this was in place, she'd focus on staff and the menu. Right now, though, she needed to make a good deal.

The club was doing renovations, apparently, and they had listed their commercial stove and oven for sale. Hope thought it looked perfect in the photos.

Someday, maybe, she'd upgrade to something French, but this looked like the perfect way to start her kitchen for now.

She'd learned that the club was closed this season during the upgrades, though it was still open to golfers.

She entered the lobby and then headed back to the kitchen. She knew her way around, she realized. It was funny the stuff that comes back to you, even after decades. The last time she was here, she'd split tips with the bartenders at the end of her shift.

"Put that in the storeroom. We can't unpack that until they finish the painting." This had to be the manager, he was ordering workers around like an emperor.

"Hello, I'm Hope Venerable."

"Hello, yes, I'm Clyde Brubaker, manager."

He walked forward, and they shook hands.

"The unit is out back."

Brubaker's short legs moved fast, and Hope picked up her pace to keep up. She'd have liked to look around the kitchen. But Brubaker didn't slow down.

They walked out to the back door, and there it was, already outside, under a tarp.

She lifted the tarp, and Brubaker stepped back as she inspected the oven / range combo.

It had six burners and a side-by-side oven. It would be in the front of the house at her restaurant. The back of the house already had ovens and a grill top. This piece would be Hope's instrument, the place she cooked in the main dining area as she would for her family and friends if they came to her home.

"It is only three years old, and honestly, it wasn't used much. The previous management didn't see the value of our full-service restaurant. We're in the midst of changing that and need something more significant. We'll be doing weddings and other large events, so this isn't the size we need."

It did look almost new. Hope felt like she might have hit the jackpot. It was worth what he'd listed it for, probably more, but she decided she needed every penny too. So, she gave it a whirl.

"I'll give you five thousand for it."

"That's five grand less than I listed it for."

"You need it out of here, and I don't see anyone else clamoring. You can't ship it. If you for one of the liquidators to take it to Detroit, you'll have to offer them a cut."

Clyde Brubaker considered her argument.

"Plus, you've got a few people here who can load it into my truck right now. I'll get it off your hands today."

"All valid points, but not five grand worth of valid points. I'll do eight thousand."

"I tell you what, I'll give you the eight, but I need you to throw that chest freezer we walked past on the way out here. Load those things in my truck, and I'll call it a deal."

Brubaker narrowed his eyes at Hope. He took a breath. The sound of drilling somewhere in the clubhouse seemed to push him to make up his mind.

"Deal. This stuff really needs to go to make way for our state-of-the-art Lancache."

"Ooh, wow, yeah, impressive. I'd love to see that when it's in."

They shook hands, and then Hope got out her new checks.

It was strange to know she had the funds to back this purchase up. Again, she felt a smile on her face. This was a lot of money, but it was for her new restaurant. *Her* restaurant!

It made her feel like her dreams were coming true, dreams diverted since she was the beer cart girl here.

"I'll get my guys to load it," Brubaker said.

She watched him wrangle a few of his staff. The stove and oven were heavy, but they had the right equipment to do the job. She made a note to make sure Dean was around later today; he'd offered his crew up to help her unload and install her new appliances.

It was a victory, this bargain she'd struck for the equipment. She knew the value and knew how to negotiate to get the best terms. Maybe she did have a knack for running a business.

She'd learned a lot from her catering jobs. Planning a budget and sticking to it was one of those skills. And without that, she'd never get her restaurant off the ground.

She'd doubted herself for decades. Sometimes all by herself, and sometimes it was Archie's voice telling her to be realistic or that she wasn't doing something right. She'd done this right. She hopped down from the back of the truck as Clyde went back inside the club.

A black Mercedes pulled up the drive and parked next to her. It made the poor pickup truck look like it ought to be in a junkyard.

A handsome, well-dressed man exited. He did not look happy. In fact, he gave the aura of never actually being happy.

Hope wouldn't have paid much attention, except he strode up to her and, by the looks of things, regarded her as if she was doing something wrong.

"What are you doing with this? Who said you could take this?"

"Take it? I just bought it."

"For what purpose?"

Instead of fighting with this pompous jerk, Hope decided to be nice. Nicer than she felt. She plastered a huge smile on her face and answered. "New restaurant downtown. You're invited to check it out once we get going."

"Downtown?" The man shifted his attention away from her and toward the back of the country club.

"Brubaker, you idiot, you're out here helping the competition! Stone is paying you to dominate, not accommodate."

"Mr. Mills, I'm sorry. What happened?" Clyde Brubaker was sputtering and obsequious to this man in the suit.

"You, you there, wait once second. You're not to leave the property with that."

"Mr. Mills, a much more state-of-the-art set of equipment is on the way. I can assure you I've just made a nice profit on the old equipment."

"That's not the point. She's opening downtown. You were at the hearing. You know that is counter to Mr. Stone's current plan for the region."

"I guess I didn't ask that. I see now. I'm sorry."

That's when Hope decided she'd had enough. "Mr. Mills, is it? I'm running late. Clyde there has my cash, and we've spent the last hour loading this equipment into my truck. So, unless you're going to unload it, I think we're all set."

Mill's jaw clenched, but it appeared he wasn't about to try to physically stop her.

Meanwhile, something clicked in her brain. Who were these two men to try to tell her anything? That she couldn't drive off with the item she'd honestly bargained to get the best price for and then paid cash to purchase.

They were not, as she used to say as a kid, the boss of her.

She got in the driver's seat as Mills continued to chew out Clyde Brubaker.

Had she snookered him in some way? No, she'd responded to his ad on Craigslist and negotiated in good faith.

But based on what she'd heard from Libby and J.J., she'd just run up against their nemesis.

Stirling Stone was determined to use imminent domain to turn Irish Hills into a rest stop. And Libby had stopped him. But maybe not for good.

It had her a bit worried that maybe everything wasn't exactly nailed down in Irish Hills. But she also trusted Libby, her old friend, wouldn't steer her wrong.

· · ·

Libby

She'd straight up lied. Libby had received an email from the grant committee, and she straight up lied in response.

"We'll be touring Covert Pier on July 3rd and will be in Irish Hills for the Fourth. Can't wait to see the progress," read the email.

"Great, see you then," Libby responded, with a boldly typed lie.

She'd let the committee think the restaurant was all set, that they'd be ready to enjoy a meal there in less than a month!

This was a big stretch of the truth, based on what she knew of Hope's progress.

Aunt Emma and her lawyer, Patrick Tate, politely sat on the porch sipping lemonade while Libby paced back and forth. She'd described the current reason she was between a rock and a hard place.

"Well, you better light a fire under your sister-friend then."

Aunt Emma had a way of solving problems by creating new ones. That said, it was Aunt Emma who'd found Hope in the first place.

If one person on the planet understood lying for a good reason to arrive at a good outcome, for a good cause, it was Aunt Emma.

Her lawyer and special friend, Patrick Tate, was accustomed to making sure Aunt Emma stayed on the right side of the law, if not always on the right side of transparency.

"Light a fire under her?" Libby asked.

"Yes, let her know you're under a deadline. Maybe she's not exactly clear about what's at stake. She gets a free building, a cottage, and rent-free, but she better start moving faster. I mean, the restaurant doesn't have a name, there's no menu listed, and I'm not sure she's hired a single waitress."

Libby had a pit in her stomach as Aunt Emma listed the things that still needed done at Hope's restaurant.

"I didn't ask her to stay at the cottage with strings attached. I'm not kicking her out."

"Of course not, heavens no. I'm just saying a little focused pressure on your part could move things along."

"Like the kind you applied to me?"

"Darling, I merely pointed you in the direction of your destiny, isn't that right, Patrick?"

The lawyer nodded in agreement, but there was a smile on his lips. He was constantly amused by Aunt Emma.

Maybe Libby would find it adorable if it wasn't Libby and her friends in the cross hairs of Aunt Emma's grand plans.

Well, it was her grand plan, too, now. Libby had bought into it lock, stock, and barrel.

Her pre-inheritance of Nora House, the master plan for the buildings Emma owned downtown, the cottages Aunt Emma had gobbled up like potato chips to stop Stirling Stone—all of it was tied in knots.

Libby was counting on the grant money to renovate the buildings to lure businesses to bring tourists to stop Stirling Stone from swallowing a fly.

It sounded like the worst campfire song of all time right now.

Libby stopped focusing on the big knot. Aunt Emma was right: One thread at a time. She needed a viable restaurant to compete with Covert Pier.

Stirling Stone had stacked the deck, again, against her and lured Chef Ellston to the competition. Hope needed to come through, this restaurant had to be ready to go, and it had to be wonderful. Libby wasn't worried that Hope could do it, but she was worried about the timing.

That was another lie. She hadn't really told Hope the stakes or the deadline.

She needed the yes first, needed Hope to be all in. But her aunt wasn't wrong. Hope should know.

"The health inspector is all set. He's an old friend of your aunt's. His family had a cottage on Vineyard Lake. He'll put Hope on the schedule as soon as she's ready." Patrick Tate piped up with that bit of news.

"That's something then. We just need her to be ready."

"That we do, that we do. Do we need to sell more jewelry?"

Aunt Emma and Libby had hocked some family jewelry to get the ball rolling on the renovations. It was how she paid for the restaurant. But that money was drying up too.

"Right now, no, but if you're sitting on a diamond broach, dust it off. You never know," Libby replied.

"Oh, that would not be comfortable."

Aunt Emma and Patrick laughed at Aunt Emma's joke; meanwhile, Libby continued her pacing.

She did not want to pressure Hope, but if the restaurant didn't move a little faster, she might have no choice.

Chapter Eighteen

Hope

The oven worked perfectly. It fit in the spot she'd allotted, and it even looked good, on display, so that Hope could cook in front of her guests. This would make the restaurant feel intimate and like a family getting together.

That was the good news.

The bad news was the menu and staff. She had neither.

She spent the afternoon on the computer, looking at logos, noodling names, and vacillating on what to serve. None of it was exactly right, and the to-do list loomed on the card table she was using as a desk in the corner where the hostess station was supposed to be. Eventually, she'd have to have an office. Ugh, more on the list.

She needed to stop waffling on what to include and start cooking.

Ooh, waffles?

No, focus Hope, focus!

She sat up from the computer and went into her kitchen.

That was it. She'd been setting up vendors, stoves, linens, and table layouts for days. What she hadn't been doing was cooking.

Hope grabbed a white apron and tied it around her waist. She pulled out the pork chops she'd snagged at the farmer's market in Adrian over the weekend.

She still didn't have her supplier locked in on that. No, no, this was time to marinate the pork, not marinate in her anxiety.

She focused on the dish.

What if she made a rosemary brine?

Hope pulled down a stainless steel bowl. It was one of the new items she'd purchased online from the restaurant supply company. She needed to have the bowl in her hands, the ingredients out, on her counter.

She paced back and forth, and looked up at the counters, out at the tables, still needing chairs.

That's it, the dish started to come to her. She grabbed shallots, baby potatoes, and some rice wine vinegar.

She put the ingredients in the bowl. She watched them shift and mingle.

She talked it out. No one was in the empty restaurant with her, but she talked it out.

It was late. There was probably no one in all of downtown Irish Hills to hear her.

So she talked it out, walked it out, and tasted her sauce.

"What if I added this?"

"Is it too mild?"

"Would this make it too tart?"

"Butter, where's the butter?"

She took the items from the stove back to the back kitchen. And she worked. This was what she'd been missing in the last two weeks since she'd come to Irish Hills. This was what she hadn't had time for. She'd been working so hard on the building, the look of things, sourcing her ingredients that she'd barely spent time behind a stove or with her fingers in a hunk of dough.

Hope was in her element when she was creating.

The tension she'd felt in her shoulders released. The process of making the dish, perfecting, tasting it, and trying it again was her dance. That was her poetry. And she needed to devote time to it. To protect that time, so the rest of her life was in harmony.

Finally, after hours of experimentation, she had it. She had a dish she'd envisioned.

But what about dessert?

Cherries were in season right now, at the end of June and only into the beginning of August, here in Michigan.

She'd make them the highlight of July.

She was letting her mind think about cherries, pacing in the back of the house, wondering how she'd use the summer fruit, when she heard a noise in the dining room.

"Hello? Anyone in here?"

She walked out to the dining room, and there was the shirtless sheriff, though this time, he was fully clothed. Greg McQueen had a nice shirt covering his nice pecs.

Whoa, where did that thought come from?

"Officer McQueen, what are you doing here?"

"Greg, it's Greg. Sorry, it's a ghost town here at night. I saw the light on, door wide open, and got suspicious."

"The door was open? That's right, I'd propped it earlier, got a new paint job up in the banquet space, trying to air it out."

"We don't have a crime rate to speak of in Irish Hills, but I still don't advise beautiful women, all alone, to leave the door open after midnight. There could be a big bad wolf, a psychotic pair of robins. You can't be too careful."

"Ah, flattery, well, thank you for checking. I'm okay. All is well."

Despite completely embarrassing herself in front of Greg twice now, she felt somehow at ease. This man had seen her be real self and still seemed to think she wasn't a lunatic.

"You know," she said, "I realize I do owe you one for saving me from the robins. Got a minute?"

"You don't owe me, but I do have a minute, just driving home. The poker game at the VFW just wrapped up."

"Great, pull up a stool."

Greg did as she instructed. There were tables throughout the restaurant, but the bar butted up to the long dining room workspace. Those diners would have the best view, Hope believed, if they were interested in how the food was prepared.

"Okay, I've been working on a good pork chop for one of my dinner entrees."

Hope pulled a white diner plate from the shelf. She knew she needed custom pottery. Well, maybe someday, that was her goal. Another task she'd get to. For now, the chunky diner-style plates worked just fine.

She opened the oven and pulled out the cast iron skillet. She judged the best chop and used her tongs to plate it.

"You're kidding. It smells so good! I never order pork chops."

"Okay, then you'll be a good recipe tester."

Hope slid him a fork, and he hesitated.

"I can't eat alone; it would be rude."

Hope grabbed her own fork, and Greg put his up. They clinked forks, and the idea of it made her chuckle.

"Okay, dig in, be honest. It doesn't help me if you lie."

Greg put the fork on to the plate.

"Make sure you get the sauce. That's key."

"Yes, ma'am."

He popped it in his mouth, and then his eyes closed. Did she kill him? There was a growl that came from somewhere in his throat.

It was nearly obscene! She laughed: This must be a hit!

"I should put the cuffs on you."

Hope blushed at that image that produced. "Excuse me?" she said.

"This is criminal. I am now ruined for all other pork chops."

"Really? You're not just being nice?"

"Ask anyone. I'm not nice." He cut another piece of the dish and popped it in his mouth.

Hope watched him eat the second bite. "Really, not too sweet, savory enough?"

"No, do not change a thing. Not one thing. This is perfect. You're amazing."

"Thank you, I don't know about that, but I do know my way around protein."

"I heard you were a good cook from Libby, but I really didn't have any idea."

"Thank you, yeah, I was catering before this. This will be my first attempt at a restaurant."

"You'll knock it out of the park. We're lucky to have you."

"Well, there, one thing down."

"What's that?"

"I have an entire menu to figure out, but at least now I know we can do pork chops one of the nights."

"Well, not this chop, this one's mine."

"Gotcha. Yes, do you want seconds?"

He raised his eyebrow at her in answer.

"Coming right up."

She'd started on a menu. Just that one dish made her feel better. She was on her way.

* * *

Hope
February 2009

She stared at the food truck. It was painted neon green and wrapped in electric orange. That didn't fit with what she would serve from it, but still, it was the inside that she knew could make or break this business.

Thanks to her girls, Hope had been to what seemed like a million high school graduation parties. The affairs had gotten more and more elaborate, just like weddings and had become over the top extravaganzas.

Graduation parties included tents, place settings, chocolate fountains, and bombastic themes. While it was once fine to slap a few burgers on the grill, put some potato chips in a bowl, and fill a cooler with soda pop, that didn't cut it these days. Some of her friends planned the graduation party the minute their kids started high school.

At these affairs, Hope had eaten her share of pulled pork, burgers, tacos, and pizza.

Her friend group of moms worked hard to keep up with the escalation, but it was a stress-filled endeavor, punctuated by the looming empty nest depression to follow.

The graduation party scene gave Hope a business idea.

Archie's house flipping flopped years ago.

They'd never moved out of their starter home. While he continued to work at several different car dealerships, he also continued to look for the next big thing.

They'd invested in a storage locker business and then a t-shirt business, and then a nutritional supplement. With each venture, money got tighter.

But Hope dug in. She was determined to bring the girls up in a nice home.

She'd renovated every square inch of their starter home. She painted, tiled, and changed out fixtures. And she did it all on a shoestring. She turned a house she was reluctant to move to into something she was proud of.

They always seemed to have next to no money, except when Archie had a new business investment idea. Then he figured out how to sink what they didn't have into the next thing that wouldn't work.

Be that as it may, she loved their little home now, and as the girls left for college, it wasn't even little to her anymore. It was a source of pride and what had kept them afloat. The bank offered them a line of credit on their home. This had become a lifeline for Hope.

That line of credit was going to turn Hope's idea into reality.

Hope planned to open a food truck for graduation parties. She had the menu figured out. That was the fun part. Then, she'd mentioned it to her mom group, and the ball started rolling fast! If she could pull it together over the winter, she had four party bookings already.

The hard part was always the money, but this time, she was ready.

The line of credit at the bank was robust and would be more than enough to start her food truck business.

She just needed to find the truck.

She'd hunted every website, classified listing, and called everyone she could think of.

It took a month of leg work, but she'd found what she needed, a used food truck for sale, and it was only two counties over.

The truck needed a good scrub down and a new paint job, but she wasn't afraid of hard work.

She'd call her new venture Venerable Events or something like that.

The truck had everything she'd need. A stovetop, a fryer, a rinsing sink, a cooler, and it actually ran! She'd checked out three trucks before this, and there were too many repairs required or not enough equipment inside, and the ones with no issues were out of her price range.

But this one, the former Fuzzy's Rolling Taco, had everything. And it still rolled. The owner had it listed for fifty thousand dollars. It was old, on the small side, and a little dingey around the edges. But she could work with all of it.

She'd walked around, tried the equipment, kicked the tires of Fuzzy's Rolling Taco Truck, and was satisfied that it was a good deal.

The final step was getting that price down a bit, and then she'd be in business. She couldn't wait.

"I'll want it. I can do thirty-five thousand."

"You're kidding. I need at least forty-eight."

That was too much, and it was over-priced. Hope knew it because she'd done her homework.

"You won't get that from me or anyone. Thirty-eight-five."

The seller looked like she'd told him his mother was a hamster. "Forty-two."

Ooh, she had him. She knew it. Hope went in with her best offer.

"Forty and I'll be back this evening with the cashier's check, drive it right out of here, and you're done. Cash in hand instead of out here getting rusty and losing value."

The seller thought a minute.

So, she pushed. "That's a good offer. People aren't clambering to start businesses in this economy, trust me."

"Deal, forty thousand cash by the end of business today."

Hope wanted to fist bump, happy dance, hoot, and holler, but she was trying to be cool.

They shook hands.

She tried not to skip back to her minivan.

She'd need to get to the bank! Her mind raced.

She'd diverted her education so long she'd given up on that dream. But the idea of earning a living doing what she loved wasn't dependent on a degree.

Ina Garten didn't go to culinary school, neither did Tom Colicchio, and he had James Beard awards. The degree wasn't important. The food was.

Once she let culinary school go, she moved forward to shape her dream career in a different way.

Even Archie was on board with the food truck idea. He'd tapped the equity of their house for one business after another, her ideas were always set aside for his. But this time he was okay with idea!

A food truck, Venerable Events. The idea had her practically speeding to the bank. She envisioned a logo, a new paint job, and weekends serving gorgeous food at area events.

She waited a few minutes in the lobby of her bank while her loan officer took care of another customer. She hoped it wouldn't take long. She needed to get the money back before the evening, as she promised.

Finally, it was her turn. Her banker, Sally Pinkle, was also a mom friend. Their daughters were all graduating this year. Sally knew her food truck plans and had been so encouraging. Even down to helping her open a special business account for the new venture.

Sally's customer had a scowl on his face as he left her cubicle in a bit of a huff. But no matter, no one was going to bring her down today.

"I found the truck, but the clock's ticking. I'm going to need a cashier's check from the line of credit so I can go get it. I talked the price down, so I'm pretty proud of that."

"Hope, uh, yeah, can you have a seat?"

Hope noticed Sally swallowing, then her lips closed into a tight thin line.

"Of course."

"So, about the line of credit," Sally said.

"Last time we talked, we had sixty thousand available to devote to this."

"The climate is changing, and banks, not just this one, have to reign in some of our credit policies."

"But the house has only gone up in value, and we've always paid the mortgage on time," Hope said.

"For some customers, we'll be switching lines of credit to loans. You tapped twenty thousand for the storage units last year. And conditions have changed, your home value, and others, are going down, in your case, it will deflate by eighty thousand."

"What? It's the same house? The bank was the one who suggested the line of credit. I don't understand."

"It isn't the end of the world, but you'll need to pay four hundred a month on the balance of your previous credit line since it's been switched from credit to loan."

In a heartbeat, they'd gone from the buffer of easy credit to an increase in their monthly debts!

"Sally, that makes buying this food truck impossible. It puts us in a worse place, financially, than we've ever been."

"It's the economy, nationally. This is impacting people everywhere. There is a bubble popping effect that is hitting everyone."

Sally said something about the subprime mortgages and recessions and how banks struggled to survive.

It was all a blur. Her dream of a food truck business was dashed. Suddenly, Hope was worried about paying the new monthly loan number.

She was worried about paying for the kids' college.

There would be no food truck business. The truck evaporated from her imagination.

Hope felt like the universe was telling her to stop dreaming these things again. It's not going to happen.

She left the bank in a fog. She got into her minivan. The entire dream was gone, in a second, with a few sentences.

Hope felt foolish. All the starry-eyed research she'd done to find the truck, the recipes she'd created to fill her menu. What a joke!

She didn't cry in front of Archie. Heck, she didn't even blame him.

He may be a crappy businessman, but he didn't cause a global recession.

She didn't cry in front of her girls; they were about to go out into the world. Their mother's disappointments weren't their burden.

But she did cry.

She cried alone in her minivan.

Chapter Nineteen

Hope, Present Day

She was so happy she could cry.

Hope walked through the restaurant. Each table, chair, and candle were placed where she'd selected. The tables would eventually have pussy willows in little milk jars as the centerpieces in spring. Then the pussy willow would switch for Forsythia or Queen Annes lace. All the wildflowers she knew were right outside the doors and along the roadsides of Irish Hills.

"You still need a name."

Hope turned to see Libby and J.J. had arrived. They both seemed just as proud as she was of how it was coming together.

"Yes, you know my catering was Venerable Catering. Maybe just Venerable's?"

"Hmm, nice ring," J.J. said.

"Well, so, now the rubber meets the road. Today's interview day."

"What's your dream staff?" Libby asked.

"I need a sous chef, probably three to five servers, a busboy, and a dishwasher."

"The former towel girl over at Hairdo or Dye, she's on the list. She was really sweet, might be a great server," J.J. said.

"I'm excited to meet Keith's son," Hope said.

"Oh, he's so talented," J.J. chimed in.

"He made us dinner the other day," Libby agreed.

"Why did it take him so long to apply? I'd have hired him on day one based on that hospitality degree from Michigan State and that work experience at Zingerman Farms."

Braylon Brady was a dream candidate in Hope's estimation.

"Keith had to give him a little push. Braylon returned to Irish Hills when his mom was sick. He'd been working at the marina since she died. Keith says they relied on each other a lot in those early days after she passed. But Keith knows Braylon's heart isn't in it. Maybe, someday, if they open a restaurant at the marina. But boat sales, storage, repair, those are Keith's thing, and his son Cole's. Braylon needs to be in a restaurant, and Keith told him this kind of opportunity doesn't come along every day."

"Beautiful! I just hope he likes me. He sounds perfect."

Hope was a little nervous about the interviews. She wanted the right mix of people in the restaurant. She knew the staff, more than any other element, would make or break the place. She poured Libby and J.J. a cup of coffee and decided to pick their brains for a moment.

"So, any advice on interviewing employees? You both seem to be amazing at mentoring people, me included. Despite my advanced age I've pretty much only been a one woman show."

"Count the number of rings they're wearing. Four rings fine, five rings, watch out, troublemaker. Take it to the bank."

Libby raised an eyebrow at J.J.

"You're wearing six."

"See, take it to the bank."

Libby chimed in, "Just trust your instincts."

"I'm good at that when it comes to making food, not so good historically speaking when it comes to business, love, or just about any other area."

"Look, we've all made missteps in life. Look at me. I nearly got myself indicted thanks to my misstep. And have somehow managed to take on the problems of an entire town."

"I thought we were supposed to be downsizing, right? At our age, instead of powering up?"

"The thing that's different now is the enjoyment of it. And the owning of our time. It doesn't take a moment away from my kids, or their school, or whatever when I work late. And I've begun to realize that guilt is just a total waste of time and emotion."

"What could you possibly be guilty of?" Hope had difficulty seeing Libby's faults; Henry, her embezzling husband, was not her fault.

"You know, I kissed Henry back in the day. I set into motion a chain of events in my life that went one way instead of another."

"Yeah, that happened to me too. I was so angry at my mother, her rules, that I went off with Archie, and boom, my path changed drastically."

"But you didn't do anything wrong. There's nothing to feel guilty over. It's just how things worked out. And now, there's a new path."

"Thanks to you two."

"Nah, Aunt Emma is the only one who really gets the credit; she saw that article on you going to the food competition. And you put yourself in that position to be at the top of your game. That has nothing to do with anyone but your own grit, sister."

"Amen to that," J.J. said.

"You're going to find the right people for the restaurant, though I move that J.J. is officially in charge of picking our romantic partners moving forward. She's the only one who killed it on that score."

"Oh, I didn't pick a winner out of the gate. I found Dean and then grew him into what I needed. In the beginning, it was, uh, let's just say he had a lot of maturing to do, and I had a lot of patience to learn. Issues in our rearview mirror are larger than they appear."

It made Hope feel better about herself that her friends knew that no one's life was perfect, despite what they posted on Facebook.

"Anyway, don't worry about the interviews. You're making *me* want to work here. Alas, I've got to get moving. Shelly's taking the day off, and I need to get to the salon."

"She's right," Libby said. "It's almost nine. Interviews are about to start. We'll let you get at it."

"How about lunch? I've got to drive to Brooklyn. Poppa's Place has great grilled ham and cheese or a cod sandwich? I'll bring us all some takeout, sound good?'"

"Love that."

"Good luck!" J.J. and Libby walked out, right past Jared Pawlak.

"Oh, look, my brother is applying."

"Ha, ha." Jared Pawlak walked in, filling his Peck's Hardware t-shirt out very impressively for a little brother they used to call pudding. Behind him, a young woman followed, sporting the same logoed t-shirt.

"Hi, Aunt J.J."

The girl hugged J.J., and then Jared made the introduction.

"This is my daughter Lila. She's here for the summers, with her mom in the winter. Anyhow. She hates working at the hardware store. Don't you?"

"Dad!"

Hope smiled. There was nothing more annoying to a teenage girl than having her parents say things. Anything.

"Well, you do. I'm not saying you don't do a good job. I'm just saying you hate it."

"Ah, well, Jared," Hope said. "I've got a dripping faucet that needs a washer back in the kitchen. Could you go look and see what size I need? And Lila and I can talk."

"Yep."

Jared made himself scarce, and Hope focused on the young girl.

"How old are you?"

"I just turned eighteen, so I can serve."

Hope did not say that she would have guessed Lila as younger than eighteen because no eighteen-year-old wants to hear that.

"Excellent. Do you really hate the hardware store?"

"Uh, my dad—no, I don't. I just have more interest in earning tips. I waitress back home, it's a Bob Evans, so not as nice as this, but I do have experience."

Lila was pretty. Hope could actually see a bit of a young J.J. in her face. Her little turned-up nose was adorable, cute as a button really, but there was something fiery inside, just like J.J.

"The plan is to be open four days a week, to start. Thursday through Sunday, and we'll do lunch and dinner. Maybe, if it goes well, next year, or the year after, we will expand to five. But I want to set us up for success with a more manageable schedule."

"I'm available."

"You'd work all four days, probably eleven to nine. You'll get lunch and a break, but you'll be busy when you're on shift."

"I'm not afraid of work."

"And depending on how busy we are, and how it works out, it could switch to lunch shift, and dinner shift kind of thing. But for now, I need a team that is all in, all the time we're open. But then three days off each week. Does that sound workable?"

"Yes, totally. I want to learn everything I can about the restaurant business and make good tips."

You and I both, thought Hope, but she didn't say it. She wanted to instill a sense of leadership, even if some of this she'd be making it up as she went.

"Wonderful. I'm going to give you the application, but I just need that on file. Fill it out, and I'll call you, probably by tomorrow."

"Thank you, will do."

In her mind, Lila was a lock. Hope conducted three more interviews and felt good about two of those candidates. Both women in their thirties gave her a great vibe. They showed enthusiasm for her restaurant concept and asked good questions about it. She had their applications and was confident that if their references checked out, they'd be great additions.

And then Camila Rojas walked in for her scheduled interview.

Camila was Hope's age, maybe older. It was hard to tell.

The moment Camila opened her mouth, it was clear that Camila was interviewing Hope, not the other way around.

She introduced herself confidently, handed Hope her resume, sat down, and then took charge before Hope had a chance to pose a single question.

"You're going to have to get the latest point of sale system. It will seem expensive now, but it will save you in the long run."

Hope hadn't even looked at things like iPad menus and checkout systems. Camila referenced the one she recommended. Hope started taking notes.

"I'm not sure you're aware, but we have almost a dozen wineries in the area. You need good relationships with them. Also, it would be nice if you highlighted local artisans here, from the art on the walls to the bowls on the table."

This was exactly what Hope wanted to do! And it was coming out of Camila's mouth as though the woman had read Hope's mind.

"So, you clearly have experience."

"I worked at Irish Hills Country Club, at Hathaway House, and was brought in to manage the expansion of Randy's Hot Dogs in Toledo, before I had to step back. I'm rooted in local cuisine but skilled in managing expanding restaurant operations."

"There is a gap here, of a couple of years?"

"My husband battled cancer for several years. I took care of him until he passed. And then, well, I've been in recovery mode since then. I wasn't sure what to do with myself. We have a place on Clark Lake. It was where he wanted to retire. I was holed up there, well, honestly stunned. Anyway, I'm ready to not be holed up anymore."

Clark Lake was about fifteen minutes' drive from Lake Manitou. Hope loved everything about Camila Rojas. Instead of worrying if Camila was a good hire, Hope worried she wasn't a good enough boss for the woman.

"I'm not going to be able to promise that you'll make anywhere near what you did in those restaurants you mentioned. I'm afraid I'm not qualified enough for you, Camila."

"I'm here for a good experience, not good tips. I've been watching your work, walking past when you're burning the midnight oil here. I want to help you build it. That's more important to me now—plus, I've had it with big cities. Irish Hills is my speed."

Hope explained her idea of only lunch and dinner four days a week and her concept of locally sourced ingredients. Camila didn't blink at Hope's ambitious plans.

"You're hired if you'll have me," Hope said humbly.

"That's why I'm here," Camila replied. "I have a good feeling about this place."

Camila also agreed to put the word out to a few of her favorite servers in the area to see if they could fill in the ranks. It was hard to find people to work in a small town, but thanks to a successful morning and the confidence of her first hires, Hope felt pretty good.

Braylon Brady was her last interview of the day.

Braylon was as handsome as his father but not gawky like the younger Keith had been. He was broad-shouldered, barrel-chested, and had a warm smile that peeked out of a rather impressive red hued beard.

"I'll shave it. That's one hundred percent fine," he said after Hope commented on it.

"You're good, you're good."

While Camila's interview focused on the logistics of running a smooth service and check out, Braylon's passion was the food.

He lit up, describing his signature dish, his favorite summer vegetable, and the things he'd learned from his experiences working his way up in various kitchens. Before Hope knew it, the interview had stretched into an hour, moved back to the kitchen. Where the two shared ideas and inspiration. They spoke the same language, even though Braylon was a quarter-century younger.

Not that he needed to seal the deal—there was no doubt Hope was lucky to have someone of Braylon's caliber at the restaurant— but Braylon knew how to get local fish, beef, and other key ingredients, right here in their own backyard.

"A friend of mine owns a distillery in Tecumseh, and they've developed a local producer in season list. It's amazing, totally useful."

Braylon showed his phone to Hope, and she looked at the list. Some were the farmers she knew, from Aunt Emma, some were new to her.

"This is what I needed; it changes the game!" It was the final piece she needed to really pull a menu together.

"If it's cool with you, I could be totally involved in helping source ingredients."

"It is cool with me."

They finished the interview with a handshake, and Hope felt like she was walking on a cloud. She wasn't alone. From her old friends to her new hires, this restaurant was happening!

She also realized she was feeling hungry.

J.J. and Libby arrived with the promised takeout lunch from Poppa's Place.

Hope gave her friends a quick recap of her busy morning.

"I'm excited. This looks good for July Fourth weekend. What a great way to start," Libby said, and Hope felt more and more like they could make it. They'd danced around that date as an opening target, but after the morning's successes, she was feeling more confident than ever.

"I don't want to jinx it, but yes, if I can get at least half the staff in here, start doing a few run-throughs, maybe."

The idea did fill Hope with nerves. That was a lot of ground to cover, but her friend was going out on a limb to give her this prime space, rent-free. Libby seemed to really want it to be open on the Fourth, and Hope wanted to come through. Even so, Hope was starting to lose sleep over pitfalls and potential disaster of disappointing her old friends with the tight timetable.

Still, Hope finished her day with a sous chef, a front-of-house manager/host, and three servers. This was progress!

The hot sun was sinking in the west by the time she arrived home. Home. She smiled to think she was referring to the old cottage as her home. The sunset did a lot of favors for the run-down cottage. It streamed in the windows and made the rooms glow, despite their lack of modern décor or lighting.

"Hello, any wild birds in here?" she said to no one in particular as she kicked off her shoes, padded into the bedroom, and made a snap decision.

It was time for another swim. Many nights in her future, she'd be tired, smell like the kitchen, and probably have aching feet, she was sure she'd plop right into bed. But tonight, she was exhilarated by the possibilities of her new venture. And if you had a clear, cool lake to take a dip in, it was almost a sin not to!

She slipped into the suit Libby had given her. She'd need to order one, but dang, Libby had good taste in clothes. Hope was more likely to grab whatever they had in the grocery store clothes aisle than to buy something of quality that would last. She worried about food all the time, but clothes? Never.

Hope walked out onto the dock and, on impulse, decided to give a shout-out.

"Hey, creeper? You home?"

"That's detective creeper to you, and glad to see you got a proper swimsuit. This isn't a nudist colony, you know." Mr. tall, gray, and handsome, Greg McQueen appeared from the far side of his side yard, beer in one hand, garden hose in the other.

"Too bad." Hope was feeling bold. She was fifty years old, long past the time when shy or timid would get her anywhere. Flexing her dormant flirting muscle, she took it a step further. "Why don't you find a suit and join me for a drink on the dock?"

"Fine, as long as you don't get fresh."

She laughed and realized, somehow, she and her neighbor shared a sense of humor. It only took a minute for Greg to join her in the lake. She stole a glance or three when he wasn't looking. Oops, she was the creeper!

They both swam a bit, splashed a bit, and sat on the dock afterward as the warm evening air and perfectly chilled wine made things too comfortable to move.

"So, not to be rude, but are you officially divorced?"

Greg wasn't being rude; it was a valid question for her. She'd come into town alone. She was building a business on her own, with no partner in sight.

"Not quite. Need to find a lawyer for that."

"I get it. Divorce is tough, even when your ex is a demon woman from hell."

"Is yours?"

"Oh, for sure, but a good mom, so you know?"

Hope laughed. She wondered if Archie was telling someone she was a demon woman from hell. On some days, she felt like it.

"I suspect there are two or three sides to your story," she commented.

"Honestly, I was a workaholic. She was sick of it. I also didn't know how to separate Job me from Husband me. So maybe I turned her into a demon from hell."

Hope knew it was all a two-way street. Archie probably could have had a better match than her. He could have lived a different life with someone else. Maybe he still could.

Hope stole a glance at Greg as they made their way to the plastic Adirondack chairs, she'd foraged out of the shed. There were a few busted slats on the chairs, but she hadn't had time to worry about the cottage décor with the restaurant taking all of her time.

Greg had a scar on the side of his abdomen. It was jagged. It didn't look like a surgery scar, though she supposed it could be an appendectomy gone sideways. She'd seen the scar when he'd helped her with the birds.

"And is that a workaholic scar?" She figured if he was sensitive about it, surely, he wouldn't be shirtless half the time.

Greg ran his hand over it. "Actually, got stabbed on the job. Put me on medical leave, and then I realized I liked not working all the time. Took my retirement out here. My wife didn't like lake life but liked her house in the right suburb that I still pay for."

"But you're back, on patrol. Still working, not retired, that I can see."

"It's a world of difference. Small town, part-time, contracted law enforcement versus, well, Detroit. That town kept me busy, let's just say. I never had time for yard work or to enjoy a delicious pork chop or go swimming at sunset."

"All pretty great things, I think."

"The biggest riot I've had to deal with over the last year is your unruliness."

"Yes, I'm a troublemaker."

"What I've learned, this time around, is that I can work, but I also have to do it on my terms. I patrol a sleepy town, hang out with a bodacious babe after work, and try to suck in my gut when I'm sitting in this chair."

Hope nearly choked on her wine while laughing.

The conversation flowed, and Greg seemed genuinely interested as she outlined what she needed to do for the restaurant.

They tossed around names, too. Venerable Foods? Venerable Café? She still didn't know.

After saying good night, she realized her daughter Julia might be a good one to ask about a name.

Julia was a writer and currently worked in social media for an entertainment company out west. She texted her oldest.

"Hey, haven't heard from you in a few days. Here's what I'm up to. I need a name for this place. Any ideas?"

"I'll think about it." Ah, good, proof of life for number one.

And then she sent a few pictures to Sara, her youngest. Who replied with a smiley emoji.

Proof of life for number two.

That was all she could ask for from one day.

Hope went to sleep relaxed from the wine, happy about her new hires, and confident that she had won the neighbor lottery of Lake Manitou as well.

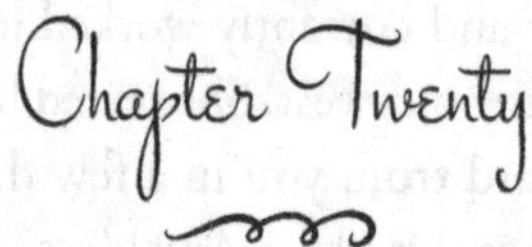

Hope

Camila had made it her mission to show up at the restaurant daily.

"I'm going to be here in the mornings, and then once we open, a little later, since we'll be working till probably ten or eleven."

After three days of interviews, Hope—now with Camila's experienced eye—finished the hiring.

Meanwhile, Braylon hunted and gathered.

"What can we source locally in July and August?" she asked, and he delivered.

"If we look for fishing operations in the Great Lakes, we may be able to do all Michigan or Canadian caught fish."

"Yes!" Her mind whirled with the possibilities of how she'd prepare her fish dishes.

Braylon found beef suppliers too. Every day, she nailed down a new recipe idea for their opening week.

Hope wanted white aprons, black t-shirts, and jeans or khakis for her staff. She'd wear the same most days. Camila had taken over sourcing uniform supplies. Lila, who was young and stylish, was enlisted as their model. To see what worked and looked okay.

"I wouldn't call this uniform fire but compared to the fugly polo shirts at the hardware store, I'm low-key happy."

Lila spoke Lila, and they just tried to keep up.

They hired two more servers, a busboy, and a line cook. Camila would seat diners and be the backup for the servers if they got in the weeds.

It was shaping up, all of it, and the days flew by.

Hope was optimistic as she and Camila worked on setting up the new ordering system.

"We're ahead of the game. I really think we're almost ready."

"I have to be honest with you," Camila said.

"Please do."

"I think you limit service to fifty the first few weeks. That's all we can handle with the current staff and experience."

"But we have space for one hundred." In Hope's dreams, one hundred people was a packed house. Crazy, but doable.

But Camila pressed on.

"Yeah, we do, but if customers come in, and have a bad experience, have to wait, get a less than stellar dish, they won't forget it. They'll share that. It's better to walk first, not run."

More than anything else, Hope wanted every single person to have a perfect night, a great meal, a beautiful atmosphere, with a welcoming vibe from the staff.

Every place was set with that intention in mind.

Hope freaking out for several hours in front of hungry and disappointed diners was not what she envisioned. Camila outlined how easily that scenario could play out if they had one hundred people and an inexperienced staff.

"I see your point." Hope was confident in her skills, but one hundred people, if they were full? She'd have to move like her rear end was on fire.

"I say, let's spread the tables out, store the extras up in the banquet area. And that way, even if you're at half capacity, it looks full. You look like a success this way, instead of chicken with her head cut off, ya get it?"

"Camila, you're brilliant. I think that works."

"Our current staff will understand our systems, and it will be much easier to onboard new people as we slowly ramp up to capacity."

The conversation was a good opportunity to bring up her other idea. The one that no restaurant in the area was doing.

"Braylon, can you come out here?"

Braylon emerged from the back of the house and joined them. Hope was relieved they had fairly big workspaces because, for a sous chef, Braylon would make a good professional wrestler, size-wise.

"Okay, here's also what I'm thinking. My goal is to source our ingredients ethically and regionally."

"We're aware. You've said that a million times, and we've known you ten or so days," Camila joked.

"I've gone over it and over it in my mind. That means my menu must be different from what people are used to."

"Well, it will be. It will be your recipes, your creations," Camila said.

"More than that, it has to change. Week to week."

Braylon smiled but also took a step backward. He'd come to understand that Camila was going to probably balk at this idea. A bespoke, ever-changing menu was more work for everyone involved.

"Lunch and dinner?" Camila squinted at Hope.

"Yes, each week we have one, maybe two lunch options, and one, maybe two dinner options. Our servers don't memorize a huge list of sides, and there are no changes or substitutions. It's one choice of protein, one side, one appetizer."

"Are you out of your mind? What if people don't want

chicken or beef or fish or want asparagus, not squash? The customer is supposed to be right, not you!"

"They're going to want it. I'm one hundred percent sure. Between my recipes and what Braylon is adding to our arsenal of ideas, they're going to want what we put on the plate."

"But if they like something, they can't come back and order it again."

"Not in the same way, no."

Camila fashioned her index finger and thumb into the shape of a gun. She then pointed it down to her shoes.

"This is you," Camila said.

"Shooting myself in the foot?"

"Right, how will you get that couple who comes every Friday for your meatloaf or whatever it is they have their heart set on?"

"They'll come every Friday for the best meal with the best ingredients at their peak."

"This is going to be amazing, and in a way, it is simpler," Braylon said.

"How so?" Camila said.

"The service will be immaculate because the servers don't have to remember fifteen special orders per table."

Braylon got it. Hope had been floating test balloons of the concept in his direction.

"But they will have to memorize your menu each week."

"I'm not a short-order cook. Braylon and I want to create unique dishes. That's why we're both in it. And every single woman we've hired is going to shine with this mission. I know it."

"I think it's brilliant. I'll do whatever I can to make it work." Braylon said.

She wanted to hug him.

"This is a learning curve, a marketing challenge, you understand?" Camila said cautiously. "We're going to have to get the word out, the Adrian Telegram, the local Facebook pages for all the lakes, like everyone needs to know what they're about to experience is unique. Still though...what if you have a dish everyone loves and wants again?"

"They can come back next time it's in season."

"You're an odd duck, Hope Venerable," Camila said slowly, then added, "Hmmm, Venerable's Bistro, Venerable Dining? It's clear we're not a diner; THAT's out now. So, have you decided on a name for this grand experiment?"

"How long do I have?" Hope asked.

"Well, you need a logo. Obviously, now I have to decide on how to publish weekly menus, so that's not the issue. But Dean Tucker said the painter for the window is here next week. Next week! Also, I want to embroider the aprons. I can do two a night. So back it out, sister."

"Okay, okay."

Hope's daughters hadn't come through with a good name. She'd have to figure it out soon.

"I'm going to call about that order of ramekins and see about getting the right printer in here. We're going to need it. A new menu every week, ugh."

Camila left their little meeting to deal with the tech end of things. Hope and Braylon made their way back to the kitchen. It was time to experiment with strawberry shortcake. Braylon was the superior baker of the two of them, Hope had discovered.

They had been working for about thirty minutes when a change in air pressure alerted Hope to someone entering the restaurant.

She turned around, prepared to sign for a delivery or let an inquiring potential customer know they weren't open yet.

Instead, she came face to face with someone who was not invited.

"What are *you* doing here?"

"Hey, this looks amazing," said Archie Venerable, her future ex-husband, as he strode into the center of the dining room. He walked further into the restaurant. He ran his fingers along a table.

Hope stood still, paralyzed for a moment, seeing Archie in this space. Her space.

"I said, what are you doing here? How did you even find me?"

Archie waved his phone at her. She saw pictures of the lake, the inside of the restaurant, all pictures she'd sent to the girls. Ugh, they'd ratted her out.

Archie put down the phone, and his face softened. "I know we have issues. I'm sorry about that. I made a mistake. I'm here to apologize. To make it right."

"Can you please keep your voice down? This my place of work."

"Aren't you the boss?"

"Yes, but that's the point. I don't want our messy, whatever this is, polluting this space."

"Polluting, that's a bit dramatic."

"Follow me." She didn't want Archie there at all. She didn't want his two cents on her business or one finger on her hand-crafted space.

"Yes, ma'am, yes, Girl Boss."

"Just boss," Hope said. Her jaw clenched as she guided Archie back outside to the sidewalk in front of the restaurant.

She didn't want Braylon, Camila, Lila, or anyone to hear whatever Archie wanted to say. She didn't want to hear it either. But maybe it was best to face this, start clean, and move on.

"Where's Bambi Carla? She give you permission to come all the way to Michigan?"

"That was a mistake, a blip. You were gone all the time. I'm sorry, you have to believe me."

"What, it's not love?"

As she talked, Archie leaned to the side. He was looking over her shoulder. He was scanning the block, seemingly taking in information about something. Even when he wasn't focused on her, he was working something else out.

"Oh, come on, don't be bitter. We've been together for

decades. We have built a family. I know what love is." He put his hand out and grabbed hers.

Hope softened a little.

The Archie leaning on the car, back when they first met, the one who listened to her about her parents, the one who didn't try to run when she was pregnant—that Archie was still there. She'd sacrificed things for Archie, a lot of things. And she supposed he'd sacrificed for their family too. He hadn't envisioned selling cars for thirty years, but he had. He paid bills, and he tried to make sure the girls had what they wanted.

They *had* built a family. She owed Archie this conversation. She just wished it wasn't here, outside her new restaurant.

"So, the girls filled you in?"

Hope should be annoyed that they'd told him where she was, but they were trying to help. Trying to see if their parents' marriage could be saved. They were used to Hope supporting Archie, their dad. Hope had never once laid her own disappointment on them. From their perspective, things were fine, fixable.

"They did. They're adamant that they want us back together, that I should be forgiven, but also, what did Julia call me? Oh, yeah, Jack Wagon. I'm a Jack Wagon and need to apologize."

Hope laughed at that characterization but then became serious. "I'm going to file for divorce. We did make a go of it; we did have good years. Decades even. But I'm done. If you want to be with Bambi, uh, Carla, go do that."

"You're being ridiculous. I'm not divorcing you. I'm here to help you!"

"I don't need your help."

"From what the girls said, you're getting this place rent-free. I did a little digging, and real estate here is about to pop off. We're in a perfection position to cash in, here, to have the business of our dreams."

Something started to come unhinged in Hope. She felt her anger rip away from the moorings that held it down over the years.

"*Our* dreams? What are you talking about?" Hope's momentary softening toward Archie evaporated. "You wanted to flip the house, own a storage facility, sell website domains, own a harness racing horse and—what was that other one? Oh yeah, alpacas! Those are just some of your dreams. You had a shot at every single one of them."

"But now we've got the capital, don't we? Smart of you to have it in a separate account for business purposes. Very smart, but think about it, we're married fifty-fifty. No prenup. Those didn't really even exist back when we had nothing, now did they?"

Hope felt cornered. It felt familiar. She was close to opening a restaurant. To doing it her way, and here was Archie, standing in the way.

"You are ridiculous, completely out of your mind. You squashed my dreams for the last thirty years, cheated on me, and now, you want to take this from me!"

"Calm down. You're acting insane," Archie said. He reached out for her again.

"CALM DOWN?" Hope was livid. For a moment, she couldn't see Archie in front of her. All she could see were spots.

She felt a tap on her shoulder. She whirled around to see Greg McQueen.

"Are you okay? Is he bothering you?" His eyes were deadly serious, and they locked on hers.

Archie did not like that question one bit. Nor did Greg appear to like Archie's hand on Hope's elbow.

"Bothering her? Get your hand off my wife!"

Hope now saw Archie squaring his shoulders, standing taller, and he pulled her by the arm toward him. As though he was the one protecting her from a stranger on the street.

The reality of the situation snapped Hope into action. She had become unhinged on the sidewalk of downtown Irish Hills.

She probably did look insane, like Archie had said. Still, she would not put it past Archie to take a swing at Greg. And she knew Greg could disconnect Archie's jaw. This wasn't good.

"Okay, no, no, no. This is my friend, my neighbor," Hope explained. She had a hand on Archie's chest.

"Detective Greg McQueen, to you."

That correction had the effect of taking Archie's bravado down one notch. He was a jerk sometimes, but he wasn't in the habit of getting arrested.

"Tell your detective friend to butt out of our conversation about our business," he growled. "It is none of his."

"Archie, give me a minute. Is that your rental car over there? Go over there and give me a minute." She was firm but had brought her voice down to a more reasonable volume.

Archie exhaled, let her arm go, and fixed Greg with a nasty stare.

Oh brother. Men.

He did, however, back up and walk back to his rental car but glared in Greg's direction as he retreated.

Hope turned her attention to Greg.

"Are you in danger?" he asked urgently. "Can you speak freely?"

"I understand what you're doing, and it's very nice, but I'm not in danger. If anyone was in danger, it was Archie. I was losing it."

"It's not nice. It's serious. I have been in situations where women are afraid to ask for my help while still in sight of their abusers."

Hope realized how much Greg must have seen in his career, how many times he'd been there in people's worst moments. She felt bad that he had to see one of her own worst moments.

"Archie has never once laid a hand on me in anger. He is not violent, and neither am I. We are, however, at some sort of crossroads. I ran from the mess he made—maybe *we* made— anyway, now I need to face what's left."

"What would you like me to do?"

"Try not to think poorly of me, now that you saw me this way, with that guy."

"I think you're spectacular, in all ways."

At that moment, Hope wanted to hug Greg. But she had Archie to deal with. She didn't want to escalate the already charged dynamic. Hope reached out her hand, took Greg's in hers, and gave it a squeeze. She hoped it reassured him that she was okay, and that she was grateful for his concern.

"I'm fine. Thank you. Truly."

She left Greg, who did not appear to want to let her go, but he did. Greg slowly headed back to his own vehicle but didn't get in it. If death stares were a thing, Greg and Archie were crossing streams in the middle of Irish Hills.

This was partly her fault. She'd skipped a step.

She had thought she was taking a break, then she'd convinced herself that she was moving on, but seeing Archie here now, she realized that coming to Irish Hills had been a kind of running away.

She needed to hash it out with Archie if she was going to create the restaurant, the life that she envisioned in Irish Hills.

She called into the restaurant.

"Camila, I'm going to have to leave for the afternoon. I've got a mess to clean up."

"I heard. You good?"

"I'm good. I just put a cart before a horse."

That was all she was going to offer in front of her staff by way of explanation.

She waved to Archie for him to follow her.

She'd take a drive over to nearby Manchester.

It was time to have an adult conversation out of earshot of anyone in Irish Hills.

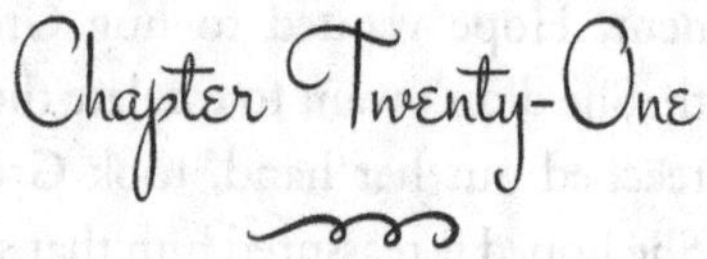

Hope

They were sitting at a booth in the Hungry Fox in Manchester.

Manchester was about thirty minutes away from Irish Hills. The drive had helped her calm her nerves.

Archie was wrist deep into a hamburger, fries, and a pop.

Hope was too worked up to eat. Despite calming herself and deciding to be an adult, she didn't have an appetite.

"The way I see it," Archie said between bites, "I manage the place. You cook. That's what you like to do anyway. The girls said your rich friend isn't charging rent in either spot, so we're sitting pretty in terms of making bank. I'll sell the Covington house, and we'll be flush with cash. How about that?"

"That rent-free thing is a temporary thing."

"Rich people love to act like they're doing you a favor. We can milk that a long time if we play our cards right."

Everything Archie said made her current friendship with Libby seem gross. She hated him knowing anything about it and even more that he wanted to take advantage of it. Hope wanted to

156

start paying rent as soon as possible. She didn't want to milk anything!

"I just want to get a divorce, okay? I don't want to run a business with you."

"Ha, well, it's more like I'm running the business, and you're running the kitchen."

Archie could turn a gold mine into a trash heap. That was his magic power. He had the reverse Midas touch.

"No. I understand the girls want us to reconcile, but that's a remnant of a fairytale childhood that I mistakenly wanted them to believe, that even sometimes I believed. But I'm not making believe anymore."

She didn't shout it, and in a way, she wasn't even saying it to Archie. She was admitting all of it to herself.

"Well, I'm sorry to hear that." Archie leaned over and produced a piece of paper. He slid it in front of her.

"What is this?"

"Divorce papers. I'm going to need a complete financial accounting of your catering profits, your contest winnings, the value of the restaurant, the cottage you've been gifted, and anything else you've been hiding."

Archie seemed to think Libby had just given her a bunch of property. He was going to be really disappointed about that. She had cash from catering and winnings, but she didn't own a thing, except the restaurant's stove.

She had zero patience with his demands.

"*You're* the one who cheated on *me*! You're suing me for divorce? That's a real laugh."

"I apologized. I told you it was a mistake. You're obviously not being reasonable. So, there are some deadlines on there. And a number to call to fax the documents. My lawyer says I'm entitled to half of this enterprise in Irish Hills. Or you can be reasonable, and we'll run it together."

"What are you doing? Every time I try to have something for

myself, you get in the way. You don't want a restaurant or to live here, or me. You just don't want to see me succeed."

"No, babe, I want what's mine, what I earned by supporting you all these years."

"That makes no sense. I supported you! All your schemes."

"Numbers on the paper. I suggest you get cracking. My attorneys are requesting a lot of information. Oh, and I know all about Stirling Stone trying to buy these places. Maybe I sell to him once I get my half."

Archie stood up, shook his head at Hope, and left her sitting at the table with the lawyer's forms and the bill for lunch.

* * *

Hope felt defeated again. She tried not to feel betrayed by her girls, who probably did just think they were helping, in some misguided way, to get their parents back together.

She was paralyzed with indecision on what to do next. Could Archie take this too? Could he force her to be a partner with him? Was everything that was hers also his? Worse, could he sabotage Libby's drive to keep Stirling Stone out of Irish Hills?

After meeting with him, she drove back to the cottage. Doubt, worry, fear, and frustration warred for a place in her head.

She crawled into bed and had a cry. It felt like she was in the same place she'd been in over and over again in their marriage, a crossroads where Archie would force the direction to take.

What were her options? Opening a restaurant was hard enough without having this drama, this roadblock in her way.

She ignored her phone buzzing. She had no doubt that word of her humiliating scene on the sidewalk had spread to her friends. She didn't want to talk about it, didn't want them all to know what a mess she'd made of things, or face anyone's pity.

When Greg knocked on her door, she lied, told him she was fine and that she just needed to be alone.

There seemed to be no way around dealing with Archie. She couldn't just throw that part of her life away. Archie, her marriage, their history, they were like tenacles dragging her down in pieces.

If she wanted to open the restaurant of her dreams, she needed to be free of him. She needed to do it on her own terms. She paced, for hours, and had no idea what time it was when the knocking started again.

This time the knocking penetrated the blanket cocoon she'd been hiding in since her confrontation with Archie.

Hope heard J.J. and Libby calling out. They let her know they were coming in whether she wanted them to or not.

"I'm okay, I promise." She said as she let her two friends in.

"Well, fine, we just needed to check," J.J. said. "We heard there was a scene on the sidewalk, and Greg said you were holed up in here. Sorry, chic. No one gets to turtle out of Sandbar Sisters ever again."

Sandbar Sisters.

Hope had thought that being a Sandbar Sister was in the past, a fun memory from her youth and not something that could turn her life around today.

But here they were.

And as much as she didn't want to let them down, as much as she wanted to be a part of bringing Irish Hills back to life, she couldn't.

Not yet. Archie was still entangled with her. She had to truly be free of him before she could make the restaurant work. She'd raced forward, she'd believed Libby's optimism, but she hadn't really cleaned up the mess that she and Archie had made of their marriage.

She said as much to her friends.

"I really want this to work, this restaurant, living here, but I have jumped the gun."

"What? Are going back to Archie?" J.J. said.

"NO, no, but I'm not sure I can pull this off, get the restaurant open by the Fourth of July and fend off *this*." She walked across the room to the table and waved the paperwork Archie had served to her.

Libby picked it up and started to read.

"Wow, he's suing you for divorce, what a jerk?" J.J. said.

"He doesn't really want a divorce. It's blackmail. He wants the restaurant. He sees dollar signs here. He wants me to do the work and him to get the reward."

"He's right, this could be huge, the restaurant, Irish Hills, if we do things fast and right," said Libby.

Hope didn't expect her friends to understand Archie. It had taken her decades to really see. "Look, I need to divorce him, get clear of that, and then open the restaurant. And maybe not here... maybe you find someone better, without such a messy personal life to deal with. I mean, maybe I bit off more than I can chew before I'm ready. Surely dozens of chefs would jump at this chance. Chefs, not housewives with baggage."

Libby grabbed Hope's hands in hers. "There's no option. We have to have that restaurant open on Fourth of July weekend. We *have* to," Libby said.

"I know you are trying to give me a pep talk, but I don't think it's going to be possible."

"I want you to do this. In fact, I know you can. That's why we came to you. But the grant committee is coming to Irish Hills on July 5th to see our progress, to compare us to Chef Ellston's restaurant in Covert Pier."

"What?" This was new information. July Fourth was a dream, a target, an optimistic goal. What Libby was outlining now was a do-or-die pressure cooker!

"We have to give her space," J.J. said to Libby.

Libby took a breath. She seemed to soften. "I should have told you why I was pushing so hard. I just can't wait a year or a month. Something has to be working there, now." Libby looked contrite.

But Hope wasn't mad at her. She'd handed an opportunity to

Hope on a silver platter. Hope just couldn't deliver; not yet, not now.

"Here's what I know. I know you'll make it happen. I know you get things done in a way that's almost superhuman. I know I'm an impediment with all this Archie stuff."

"Look, no matter what, you're our friend. I understand if you need to back away. You have to do what's right for you. I should have been transparent. But, well, I didn't want to scare you."

"It's the truth," J.J. added. "What we're trying here, it's uh, well, it's not for everyone. I'm a townie who loves this place, and I think it's impossible half the time."

Hope walked over to the kitchen table. She'd had this feeling before. She'd watched her visions evaporate. But there was nothing she could do to stop it. And if it really was that critical to the entire town, she didn't want everything to hinge on her screwed-up relationship with Archie. That wasn't fair to anyone.

She thought of the staff she'd assembled, the menu she had begun to craft, and even the vendors she'd met so far. All of it was slipping through her fingers.

"We shouldn't have put this all on you. I feel like I'm no better than Aunt Emma. She snookered me into this entire mission," Libby said.

All three ladies were now sitting at the table, trying to piece together what was next.

"Oh, Aunt Emma, she's an evil mastermind," J.J. said.

That put a smile on Libby's face.

"Remember the save the Dance Pavilion thing you did, with the roller skating?" Hope said. This situation was the same but on steroids.

"Yeah, funny story that. I own that too and have to figure out what to do with it." Libby put her head in her hands.

"You're not alone. Me, Dean, Keith, we got ya," J.J. said to Libby.

"I know, thank you. I'm just sorry that I railroaded you, Hope."

Hope didn't feel railroaded by her friends. What she felt was saved. She'd had nothing but joy since they stepped back into her life.

Her life. Her dream.

She'd let those things be diverted, changed, muted for thirty years. Over and over again.

She sat up straighter in her chair. An idea came into her head. But she had no idea if it was legal or possible.

The people at this table were her future, a new kind of family. Sure, she loved her girls. They had a place here, too, if they wanted it. But Archie, not so much.

He shouldn't be the one to decide what came next in her life.

"Who's that attorney your aunt uses, the one that seems like he's in love with her?"

"Patrick Tate," Libby said.

"Yeah, do you have a lawyer? If not, he'd be good at looking over this stuff Archie handed you," J.J. said.

"No, I don't have a lawyer, but I do have an idea."

"Okay, well, let's call Patrick," J.J. said.

"If this works, you might be stuck with me," Hope said.

"I don't know what you're planning, but that was the point all along," Libby smiled.

And the fire came back into her friends' eyes. The fight that saved a dance pavilion when they were kids was contagious. Maybe Libby had passed it on to Hope.

Hope was sure of one thing. Archie wasn't going to decide what she did anymore.

He wasn't going to get to stop her dreams before she had a chance to make them come true.

Chapter Twenty-Two

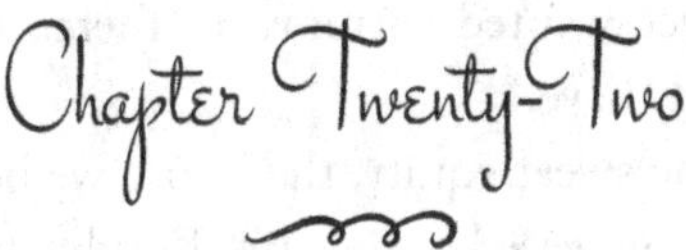

Hope

To win big, sometimes you had to risk big.

That always seemed like a line of bull crap to Hope, especially when Archie was risking their future at every turn, with every stupid scheme.

But maybe there was truth to it.

Hope was about to take a risk.

Archie had agreed to meet Hope at Patrick Tate's little office around the corner from her restaurant. Her restaurant. She was manifesting left and right since she decided what she was going to do about Archie and her divorce.

She slid the piece of paper to his side of the conference table.

"What is this?"

"It's a settlement."

"A settlement?"

Hope watched Archie as he read. His lips moved.

She decided to help him out. "Thanks to a red-hot housing marking, you're sitting on a house that is worth three hundred and fifty thousand dollars. You'll remember that we purchased it for just under one hundred grand. Not a bad turnaround. Sell it, keep it. Do what you want. I'm signing it over to you."

"We wouldn't have that house if it wasn't for me," Archie replied. "You never wanted to move in there. You're giving me something I already have."

"Thanks to my sweat equity, the house we bought with both of our savings has increased quite a bit. I'm the one who turned it into what it is. As the kids say, I have receipts."

"We have a mortgage," Archie countered.

"Last I checked, we only owe thirty grand on the mortgage, even after all we went through during the recession. You're sitting pretty there with a ton of equity."

She knew her numbers, she knew the market, and she knew that she was giving up something that, if she went to court, she'd likely win half of.

Patrick Tate had drawn up the papers, even though he thought this was a bad idea. Poor Patrick was used to women ignoring his advice though, and no lawyer would advise their client to do what Hope was doing.

It was a huge risk.

"So, the house I have, I keep, big deal."

"Archie, you don't want to be with me, and I don't want to be with you. We've raised two amazing daughters. We had some good times, but you're going to go your way, and I'm going to go mine."

"That restaurant? You're no Chef Ellston. That thing is going to tank unless you have my help."

"I appreciate you want to help, but I want to try it, all on my own. To seal the deal, to have you sign that other paper."

She slid a check across the table this time.

He read, and she helped him along.

"I do not want alimony or support. Just take it all, and we're done."

"What if I want alimony?"

"I've talked to several lawyers. You cheated. That falls under marital misconduct. I have proof. In addition, I gave up many career opportunities to raise our children, sacrificed my education, and also pulled out of the food truck business to support you and us. I will bring all of this up and get half plus support. It's a sure thing. Also I've got screenshots of you and Bambi Carla."

"You just got that cottage, that restaurant—you're hiding money! You're the liar!"

"Check these, show them to a lawyer, whatever you need." She pointed to the deeds to the restaurant and the cottage, which were still firmly in Emma and Libby's names. "I've been given nothing but a place to stay for a few days. Sorry, you got the wrong impression on that."

"That restaurant could be a gold mine."

"Well, you could do it with me, but just so you know, one in three restaurants fail in the first year. So, you can have half of a hugely risky new business or all of our old house and zero obligation to pay alimony."

Archie had no easy reply, no sarcastic comment. He looked at the paperwork and back up at Hope. Archie picked up the pen. He signed the settlement and then signed the second agreement.

That second agreement was finely crafted, thanks to Patrick. Hope agreed to give Archie the house, and she also agreed to waive any claim to spousal support. For his part, Archie agreed that he had zero claims to her business, her winnings, her ideas, her recipes, to anything she did moving forward.

Hope was giving up security, what she was legally entitled to in a divorce, to gain complete freedom from any more entanglement.

She knew Archie would take it. He would rather take the quick cash, the get-rich scheme, rather than do what it took to build something long-term. The restaurant was going to be a long game.

She was right.

"This is it?"

"This is it, except you know, maybe if the girls ever get married and have kids, we'll be at birthday parties or something." She smiled at Archie. He was why she had two wonderful girls. For a time, it had felt like Archie and Hope against the world.

Archie blinked. He seemed a little stunned. Stunned in the same way he looked when she told him she was pregnant. Things were changing in their lives, big things. Their lives always seemed to take a sharp turn, never a slow curve.

"I am proud of you," Archie said. Hope felt a lump in her throat where bile had been only a day ago.

"Thank you."

"And your mom was wrong. You were the prettiest bride I'd ever seen. I didn't get hitched just because you were knocked up."

Hope laughed, and with it came a huge relief. The weight came off her shoulders. Her future was clear, even though a few tears now clouded her vision. She hadn't expected that when she went to make the deal of her life.

She stood up, walked over to his side of the conference table, and then kissed him on the head.

This was done. They were done, but it hadn't been all bad. Whatever bitterness she'd felt against him melted into the batter.

Her choices weren't always his fault. Sometimes it was just the way things were.

But now, there were no kids, no husband, no blue pregnancy stick that would change her direction.

She was betting on herself, her food, her dream, and for the first time ever, she felt like the odds were in her favor.

The house, and spousal support? They were a small price to pay to follow the biggest dream of her life.

Quitting was the risk, giving in was the risk, and not trying to make this dream work was the risk. Regret was the risk. One she wasn't willing to live with.

Hope was ready to make this dream work, with nothing or no one in her way.

Chapter Twenty-Three

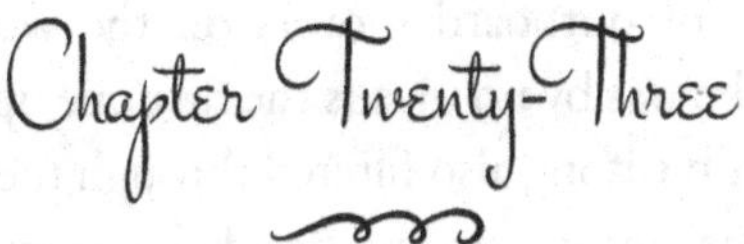

Hope

One more thing, she needed one more thing. They'd have fish from a charter fishing company on Lake Huron, they'd have first of the season cucumbers as the side dish, and Braylon had come up with a great idea on an elevated strawberry shortcake.

They were all working non-stop, but Hope was having the time of her life. The staff worked hard too, and it felt like they were coming together as a team.

One week before the official opening day, July Fourth, they were doing to a test run. They'd prepped what they could, the staff all planned to be there for their first full shifts, and the restaurant would be filled with friends and family.

The plan was to iron out kinks in the kitchen and with service, on a friendly audience. Hope planned to do everything that day exactly as she would if they were actually open.

She tried to sleep in a little, not too much, but a little.

Her days would soon be a whirlwind on the four days she was

open. She estimated she'd be at the restaurant long after the last dish was washed.

Still, she was too excited to sleep past eight. It was a sunny day in late June. This was a full-on busy season on Lake Manitou. From the sound of outboard motors on the water outside she could here that she was by no means the first one up.

The music of birdsong also filtered through the open windows in the little cottage. She got up and decided to immediately put her bathing suit on. What was the point of living on this lovely lake if not to take a swim first thing?

She wrapped a beach towel around her waist, padded out to the end of the dock, and looked around. Later, there'd be pontoon boats, speed boats, and jet skis motoring by, but at this hour, all she spied were a few fishermen quietly jockeying for spots to find the day's score.

One fisherman was close enough to trigger the lake wave greeting.

The lake wave: If you know, you know, Hope thought, with a smile on her face.

The fishermen returned their focus to their quarry. Hope braced herself for the water.

"No time to dawdle. Let's get moving."

She jumped in. Her body sank down to the sandy bottom, and she was awake! From toes to forehead, she was awake. It was faster than coffee!

She swam to the surface. It took her ten minutes to swim to the dock, two cottages over, and ten minutes back. It was the perfect way to gently move her body and warm her muscles. But it was also her mediation, her focus. She cleared her mind. She knew she'd be making decisions all day, new ones, and familiar ones. But for twenty minutes, there were no decisions, just peace as she focused on each stroke. She reached her arms out long, and she kicked her legs in time with her arms. Over and over, this was her meditation.

She was ready.

Hope returned to her dock, a little winded but alive, awake, and excited to take on her day. As she climbed out, there was her towel, ready and waiting to be wrapped around her body by her neighbor and erstwhile bodyguard.

Greg held open the beach towel, and Hope stepped inside. She grabbed the ends and wrapped herself up. Greg stepped back.

"That's some high-end concierge service for a tiny cottage rental."

"I do what I can."

"Thank you."

"You're having a huge day. I wanted to wish you luck."

Greg had stepped in when Archie was at his most Archie. She wasn't in any danger, and the entire thing was so embarrassing, but also it made her feel something new about her neighbor. He was a flirt, a little bit of a pain in the neck, but ultimately, he seemed to have interest in her that might go beyond neighborly.

That said, he'd never crossed the line, made her feel rushed or uncomfortable. She was in the midst of a divorce, starting a new business, and in limbo in many ways. Greg was a possible part of her future, but he hadn't complicated anything. He'd just made it all a bit sweeter.

"I want to show you something," he said as she toweled off.

"I may be naïve in a lot of ways, but that's a line I'd tell my girls to pass on."

"You've got the dirty mind, not me."

"What then?"

"It's right here, on the other side of my cottage. Check it out."

Hope followed Greg back up the dock across her lake frontage over to his. His cottage was a mirror layout to the one she was in. But he'd added new siding, new roof, new landscaping. All of it gave her ideas of what she could do if the next part of her plan worked.

She had a lot to accomplish before then.

Greg led her up into the grassy area of his yard, slightly to the side, where the tree line provided shade.

"Where in the world are you taking me? I do have stuff to do today, you know?"

She said it lightly, though. This season in her life might turn hectic, but she wanted to be a person who appreciated all of it. Even the handsome neighbor with a towel and a goofy secret to share.

They stopped, and he stretched his arm like a Price is Right model. "Look!"

He was pointing to the grass. It took a second to register what she was seeing.

"Morels!"

"Yep, I was getting ready to kill some weeds up by the house and walked out here last night to find this little crop."

"No one could find any for us when I created the dish for tonight!"

Morels were a delicacy. They were found all over Michigan but unpredictably enough that you had to hunt for them. She had an idea of how to serve them but never had the time to really hunt in the midst of all the other work she'd done.

She chalked it up to another fun thing to find as her restaurant menu evolved.

"Wild foraged morels are hundreds of dollars per jar."

She bent down and picked one. She ran her finger over the soft ridges.

"I have a basket in the shed. I'll fill it while you're getting ready; the first bushel on the house. Sound like a deal?"

"I mean, yes!" It was getting later, and she did have several other stops to make for ingredients before she started prepping for service.

Hope spontaneously wrapped her arm around Greg and kissed him on the cheek. For a moment, he held on, and so did she.

She caught herself. And realized she wasn't ready for full-on romance yet.

"All this time, all I needed to do to impress girls was find wild fungus. Who knew?"

Hope laughed. The little spark would likely grow between them, but he was sensitive enough to understand and to let her take the lead.

"Thank you, neighbor," she said.

"You're welcome, Chef. Now, go get ready. You're still soaking wet."

She turned and walked back to the cottage, the word 'chef,' music to her ears, and the idea of morels fired up her fevered food imagination.

As mornings went, this one was darn near perfect.

* * *

Her guinea pigs included Jared Pawlak, J.J., Dean, Libby, Keith, Aunt Emma, and Patrick Tate.

They'd helped her recruit Keith's other son, Cole, Arrow Orwig, who owned the gas station, Clyde Brubaker's mother, the entire town council of Irish Hills, and Mayor Chet Eastland.

To round it out, Keith and Dean had roped in several members of the Local VFW.

They had two dozen people at the tables.

Hope had really wanted fifty to test their mettle, but two dozen was still a good number for this dress rehearsal.

They had a few hiccups; one server spilled an entire tray of food.

The point of sale didn't want to connect to the Wi-Fi.

And the dishwasher got behind, even with that smaller capacity test run.

Most importantly, though, the food and the atmosphere seemed on point.

Hope started them off with her version of the charcuterie board. She called it the Nosh Plate. She envisioned the items on the Nosh Plate, like the rest of the menu, would shift and change as the season moved from the late spring to the heat of summer to the burnished warmth of autumn.

Each table had water, and the staff suggested pairings of wine for the upcoming meal. Hope inspected the appetizers, about to go out, as the servers poured the wine.

"I still cannot believe we don't have a soda fountain in here," Camila said.

But instead of a soda fountain, they had hand-selected wines from Lenawee County and some from Leelanau, up north.

Beer? Well, they had that too, but not flights. Just seasonally appropriate microbrews. If Libby wanted a pub in Irish Hills, she'd have to figure that out. Food, not hops, was Hope's passion.

This was the first time her guests would encounter the idea that they had no choice.

This limited selection was the risk. It wasn't up to them what was on the plate. It was up to the chef.

Her diners would have to trust that she would find the best ingredients at the perfect time, prepared with love, and care every time. They were in her hands, and she would give them the best meal of their lives. She would chase that goal every service, and hopefully, her diners would trust her to do it.

Hope listened in as Lila explained the Nosh Plates.

"We start off today with local basil and herb cheese, stone-fired crackers created by Chef Venerable, a few pickles and peppers from Tony Packos of Toledo. Also, enjoy the bread, our sous chef, Braylon Brady, created especially for tonight. Feel free to eat it plain, or my favorite, with the dipping sauce on your table. It's so good."

Good, perfect, Hope thought and then turned her attention to the next step. She focused on each salad plate coming up to the counter as the guests oohed and aahed over the Nosh Plate. Meanwhile, Braylon supervised preparation of the lettuce wedges for today's salad.

As the salads went out, Hope's main course began to heat up. Braylon would handle the side dishes, but it was Hope who cooked twenty-five whitefish. Each would need to leave her skillet with consistent temperature and flavor. She needed to be fast, faster than if this was a beef dish. Fish didn't take long. She did a dance between the range and the oven. She used her tongs to test, move the dishes around, and test again.

"Plating main."

She called out, and her staff was there, ready with the dinnerware. She'd get the fish on the plate, and they'd arrange the sides and the garnishes.

Hope wanted each plate to not only taste delicious but look beautiful. Not fussy or overly done, but beautiful. They'd practiced several arrangements, but today, Queen Anne's Lace garnished each plate.

Braylon showed her the first tray, filled with plates for their very first table.

Hope looked it over.

"Each one, like this one." She pointed to the plate she liked the best: Zero mistakes, balanced, seasoned, and still hot.

The first plates went out, but Hope didn't have time to revel in it or gauge the room. She was thinking of desserts. She was so in the zone that she almost forgot.

Luckily, Camila remembered.

"This would be a good time."

"Yep, on it."

Braylon took the tongs from her hand, and Lila handed her a glass of white wine. Braylon slid in behind the range and took over as Hope stepped from behind the counter and into the restaurant.

She took a deep breath. Her guests were smiling and laughing, and the sounds of happy surprise at the bites they were taking played like little piano keys.

For a second, she didn't know if she could do it. She didn't know if she could speak, share her feelings, or express the gratitude bubbling over like the saucepan on her range.

But she had to find the words. She had to find a way to let them know how special this was to her, how special they were.

She lightly tapped the wine glass with a butter knife.

"Hello, welcome to my restaurant. I'm Hope Benton Venerable. I just want to take a moment to thank you all for taking time tonight to help me do this, to help us all iron out our dinner dance here. And beyond that, I want to thank you for opening up your homes, your businesses, and your hearts, to my idea of this restaurant. I don't know how it's going to go, what people will think of it. But I do know, tonight, I'm doing my best to show you how much I appreciate you by preparing the best meal I know how. That will be our goal every night. So enjoy! And cheers."

The room of familiar faces and new friends raised their glasses and responded in kind with a hearty cheer.

Then a question from her diners interrupted her return to the stove.

"Do you have a name, you know, so we can tell our friends?" The bold question came from J.J., of course.

Hope had avoided naming the place. She had some superstition that naming it would jinx it or make it go away. The menus had no logos, and the awning outside remained empty. But it came to her at that moment.

"Hope's Table." The words caught in her throat a little. It had come to her in that instant.

That was it. That was the name. All this time, they'd toyed with the name Venerable—it was such a good last name, so perfect for all her other endeavors—but here, Venerable didn't fit. Hope did.

They had the rest of the main course to plate, and dessert to serve, and dishes to wash, and an assessment of their strengths and weaknesses to sort through. But at that moment, with those glasses raised, Hope very much felt her dream of thirty years become a reality.

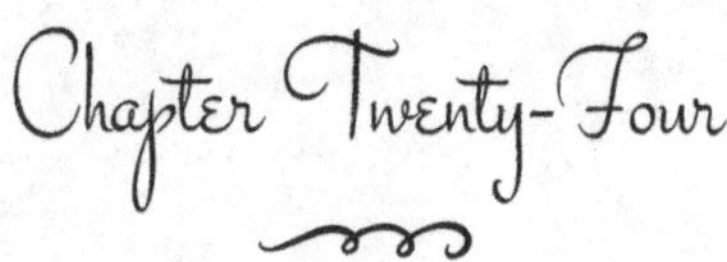

Chapter Twenty-Four

Libby

Libby prepared an agenda. Representatives from the grant committee had spent July 3rd and 4th in Covert Pier. Two days, and a wonderful time, apparently.

They had decided to drive to Irish Hills in the morning.

The committee had seen videos, read Libby's plan, and had questions for her throughout the process of trying to secure the grant. Visiting the two communities vying for the grant money was the final step in their selection process.

Keith had stepped up, and they were meeting at his marina. The place was hopping for a holiday.

Figuring out what to wear on a holiday where you were all business but showing off the charm of your casual small town lake resort was like solving a Rubik's Cube. Darn near impossible.

Libby opted for a pair of boyfriend jeans, cropped at the ankle, a white sleeveless t-shirt, and a lightweight cardigan. She used to look down her nose at capris. They were a fashion garment that screamed, *I can't commit to shorts or long pants!* They were the tankini of pants! But now, she loved hers. She didn't have to worry about a tan or errant spider vein and could still look somewhat casual. The fashion land mines for women were legion.

Keith was busy helping boaters. The big rush was in the morning, but now, at noon, several boaters who didn't have cottages to dock at were returning to the marina. It was a hub of activity. Libby watched Keith smile, help boats dock, answer questions. For a moment she forgot the whole point of the day. All she could think of was how happy she was to be here, in his life, at this point in hers.

She blinked, dabbed a little perspiration from her upper lip and refocused on the business at hand.

A hot day in July on Lake Manitou was peak Pure Michigan. The sun was going to help Libby make her case.

After a flurry of gassing some, docking others, and answering the odd question, Keith found Libby pacing on the side of the marina building.

"You're going to do fine. What's not to love here?"

"Right, right, it's just this grant money was key for convincing the city council to hold off on Stone Stirling's plan. If I don't get it—"

"—It's going to work out, and why the long pants? You have great stems. It's a real shame."

Libby laughed; Keith was good at getting Libby out of her head.

"Stop. I'm going for resort intimidating. It's a tough look to pull off."

Keith gave her a little swat on her backside, and she punched him in the shoulder.

Sometimes she fretted about the decades without him in her life, but he had a life he'd loved in that time. For the most part, so did she. She had to be content that they'd found each other again when they were supposed to. There was a rightness to the timing.

"The marina is crazy busy," Libby observed.

"Yes, well, I'm down a staff member thanks to Hope poaching my son so he could learn more about poaching eggs or whatever."

"She says he's gifted, and that's saying a lot. She has an amazing way of food. She says he comes up with solutions when she's stumped and has been key in finding local vendors."

"He takes after his mother more than me," Keith said. Keith's wife had died several years ago, but it touched Libby deeply to see how Keith honored and remembered her.

Her warmth was visible in him and in their sons. Wherever she and Keith were headed, as friends or as partners, she was grateful to Keith's wife. Libby believed she'd made him a better man, and left his life with more to give, instead of depleted. Libby wished she'd have known her.

She hugged Keith. His presence, J.J.'s, and her aunt's all helped her remember that it was the people here that inspired her to fight for the place.

"Okay, show time. I think that's them."

Libby took a deep breath.

"Relax, Irish Hills practically sells itself."

"Yeah, well, it sure did to Stirling Stone."

A man and woman got out of a rented SUV. They two committee members had volunteered to spend their holiday traveling around, visiting Covert Pier and Irish Hills.

"Welcome to Irish Hills."

"Libby, so great to meet you in person. I'm Nancy Benner and this is Martin Hoskins."

They shook hands, and Libby introduced them to Keith.

"This is Keith Brady. He owns Steve's Marina."

"Not Keith's Marina?"

"Bought it when Steve retired, didn't want to print new t-shirts." Keith wore his work uniform, a vintage Steve's Marina t-shirt, and shorts.

"Makes sense."

As planned, Keith captained his boat, and Libby narrated a tour of Lake Manitou and the connected Round Lake.

She pointed out the history, the homes, the row of vintage cottages, the old hotel, now shuttered, and explained the plans underway to restore, not bulldoze the unique homes.

The lake was packed with skiers, boaters, and every type of watercraft you could imagine.

As Keith said, this part of the tour sold itself. They spent about an hour on the lake, which didn't disappoint. It was beautiful and vibrant, and Libby's only regret was not telling the committee to bring bathing suits so they could jump in for a swim.

Libby thanked Keith for the boat ride, and now, on to phase two of her tour, Downtown Irish Hills. She would have to make the development plans she'd shared with them in emails and renderings come to life.

The lake was the easy part. People loved Lake Manitou, Round Lake, Loch Erin, Wampler's, and Vineyard. They were coming in larger numbers to the fifty-plus lakes that surrounded Irish Hills.

But there wasn't much to do in Irish Hills proper. That was her challenge. In fact, the town hadn't been able to recover from the 1989 tornado that leveled so much of it. The rest of the area towns had moved on. Irish Hills had not.

Libby was there to prove they could and should.

Libby had taken the sides and hardtop off her Jeep Wrangler. It was a beautiful day for the open-air ride, and Libby wanted to be sure to take advantage of it.

They drove into town, and Libby pointed out the renovations at the local gas station, courtesy of her old friend, Reginald Bellamy. He'd come through when she needed him, in a big way.

They rolled by the town square, which Dean Tucker had beautifully restored. Libby didn't say a word, but Nancy Benner, an expert in the beautification of public spaces, noticed the flowers planted in the square.

That was all Aunt Emma and her Floral Beautification

Committee. While Libby negotiated with contractors and sweated over the business plans, Aunt Emma had harnessed the men and women of her retirement home to plant flowers almost everywhere. They'd added huge potted arrangements every twenty feet along the sidewalk, and she'd convinced Jared Pawlak to help her hang baskets on the newly installed light posts.

They were details that Libby didn't have time for, literally, and as she drove into town, it nearly made her cry with joy. There was still so much undone, so many plans unfinished, but darn if Aunt Emma's flowers didn't make everything look gorgeous.

Libby swallowed and worked to restore her professional sales pitch demeanor to the committee members.

"This is the main concentration for the grant funds. As you can see, we have a stretch of buildings here, with renovations well underway and completed, in the case of the restaurant." Libby pointed out, with pride, the five connected structures they'd worked to renovate since she started.

"What about across the street?" Martin asked.

There was a similar stretch of buildings that ran parallel along Irish Hill's downtown area. They, too, needed development, ideas, tender loving care, and/or a sledgehammer.

"We're investing everything we have into the lakeside. And we're confident that, with the help of your community development grant, and the new businesses clamoring for these premium spots, the second piece to revitalizing Irish Hills will be less about grants and more about the obvious demand to open right here. Once we show what's possible, we will be able to grow privately. The grant will put Irish Hills in a position to thrive and prompt planned growth."

Libby took a breath, then tried to turn their attention back lakeside. "Renowned chef Hope Venerable is the restaurant's proprietor that anchors the lakeside space. She just opened it. I think you'll find it is a singular dining experience."

She knew they were competing with Chef Rami Ellston's flagship restaurant. The Food Channel was reportedly in talks to do a series with him about his restaurants. It was a lot to compete with.

As if on cue, Nancy gushed, "Oh, you should have seen what Chef Ellston had on the menu! Delicious, and then, of course, Mira Low was there. They apparently are getting married somewhere in Covert Pier! Can you believe it?"

"Oh, terrific. Quite glamorous." Libby was obliged to feign happiness upon hearing how well her competition was doing. But a pit in her stomach started to form. With Ellston's restaurant, the star power of a TV show, and a supermodel deciding to get married there, Irish Hills wasn't going to be able to compete.

"Oh, and her brother was there too," Nancy added. "He is so handsome. You can see why he's starring in that new Elvis movie."

Libby listened as her two passengers exchanged notes on the celebrity encounters from their trip to Covert Pier. There was zero chance of them running into a supermodel or movie star in Irish Hills. Zero.

But she knew Hope had created something unique and lovely with her restaurant. She knew Dean Tucker had renovated each building with care. They had a diamond in the rough. She just hoped the committee could see that.

The typical traffic of Irish Hills was two cars and a kid on a ten-speed bike, even on July Fourth weekend.

Libby ushered them to the restaurant.

Hope did not disappoint.

Every meal here was unique, fresher than anything Libby had ever tasted, and you just felt good, cared for, indulged in the best possible way. Time slowed down at Hope's Table.

"Oh, my goodness, I've never had these before. What are they?" Martin Hoskins, the other part of the dynamic committee duo, was talking with his mouth full.

"Morel mushrooms, they grow wild here, but they're elusive;

in fact, it's the last week for them," Hope explained, then took care of the rest of their foodie questions before heading back to the kitchen with a confident, "Enjoy."

Libby answered every other question about Irish Hills. She hoped her plans won them over.

Certainly, Hope's food had to have. No celebrity chef or celebrity chef's girlfriend and her celebrity brother could match what Hope had pulled off in this space in such a short period of time. The restaurant was fairly empty, so that meant they got all the attention, and the food and drinks came immediately to the guests that were there.

Libby was proud of Hope, amazed by her, and so glad Aunt Emma had found her.

Now, if the darn grant committee would just give them the funds, there'd be no stopping her from holding off Stirling Stone. It would be impossible for him to argue for the bulldozing of Irish Hills if they had a viable little commercial district here.

They finished their meals with a delightful raspberry tarte, prepared, they'd learned, by Braylon.

Every dish was carefully arranged and then melted in your mouth. Hope also let Nancy and Martin know that even the plates they used were one of a kind from a local Michigan ceramic artist.

It was a much smaller crowd than the test run. In fact, there weren't even four tables full of diners—but that's okay, that's okay, Libby reassured herself, that meant great attention to each customer.

Libby had to work on that next: Getting people to Irish Hills. Ugh, one crisis at a time.

Her guests took a walking tour, and finally, her sales pitch was complete. Nancy Benner and Martin Hoskins were on their way back to Lansing, Michigan, to decide the fates of two small towns.

There was nothing left but to wait.

* * *

Two days later, trying to enjoy her lunch at Hope's Table, Libby was seated at the bar, watching her friend cook her heart out. Libby's phone vibrated. There was a new email in her inbox.

She unlocked the screen and held her breath.

The subject line, "Grant Award," had her heart beating fast. This was it!

Libby clicked it open and read through niceties as fast as she could. Then her eyes hit the line that she'd been looking for:

As much as we enjoyed our time in Irish Hills and believe you are on the right track for community redevelopment, your project is newer, less well defined, and unfortunately not as poised to make the maximum use of the funds. The number of people dining at Hope's Table had the committee concerned that the funds toward your project will have less impact, seeing as fewer people visit Irish Hills than Covert Pier. Please know that you are welcome to apply next year once your project is at a further stage.

The air went out of Libby's lungs. That was it. She'd failed! Stirling Stone had won! She'd done a lot for Irish Hills...but not enough.

Almost as if on cue, or like there was a hidden camera in the restaurant, a man sat down next to her at the counter.

Stirling Stone.

"I'm assuming you got the email, tough break."

"Am I on *Candid Camera?*"

"Ha, no, but my attorney informed me that the word went to the winner about an hour ago."

"Of course."

"This restaurant is divine, truly, and you pulled off so much, so quickly. But I'll tell you, Chef Ellston, it's really incredible. He's decided to take over the entire block in Covert Pier, he's buying up space there left and right. He's on track to do for Covert Pier what the Gaineses did for Waco, Paula Deen for Savannah, or The Pioneer Woman in Oklahoma, that kind of thing."

"Terrific for them."

Libby wanted to punch Stirling in his perfect face. But she realized that would be a bad idea. He'd probably sue her, and she didn't have the money for that right now.

"You know, I could take over, take this town from here."

"Taking over every town in Michigan, are you?"

"Oh, I didn't take over Covert Pier, I just introduced the possibilities to Chef Ellston."

"And also dangled a Vegas restaurant in front of him," Libby said.

"I know a good thing when I see one, no doubt."

"Maybe you should jump in the lake. No wait, I want to keep the lakes clean and free of toxins."

"I understand you're emotional. If I were you, I'd reconsider the offer. We're really on the same team."

Hardly. Stone and his group wanted to tear down the downtown, put in a massive travel plaza, and bulldoze all the old cottages and homes along the shores of Lake Manitou!

She'd seen his hotels and resorts. They were big, slick, and corporate. He wanted to bring that Big Slick Energy to their quiet resort community. Aunt Emma had literally put her entire fortune on the line to stop it. And now, Libby was there, on the front line doing the same.

"Like I said, to be cliché about it, take a long walk off a short pier."

Had she just said that? Long walk off a short pier? Ugh, her anger had muddled her thinking.

Stirling Stone laughed...and then Hope handed him a bagged lunch!

What the heck?

Hope shrugged. "He called ahead."

Libby was infuriated. Stone had helped sink their chances by propping up Chef Ellston and his new venture in Covert Pier. They weren't playing on an even field. But of course, when billionaires were involved, that was always the case.

Libby usually had a plan with a list and a list of plans. This time she was stuck. A huge part of her efforts depended on getting that community redevelopment grant money.

She didn't want to break the bad news. She didn't know what do to next. She'd been so confident that they'd succeed.

But the grant was going to Covert Pier.

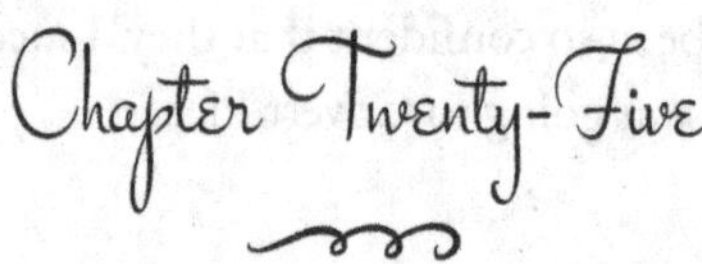

Hope

It was Hope's turn to give the moral support. She had come to Nora House with a Domino's Pizza. There were times a girl didn't want to cook. Also, Domino's world headquarters was in Ann Arbor, that qualified as local.

J.J. was headed to Nora House in a bit with wine, but Hope wanted to do this next deal before their third friend arrived. She suspected she'd have to twist Libby's arm.

Though Libby was generous, and never once did anything that made Hope feel awkward about accepting that generosity, it had been weighing on her. How could she stand on her own two feet if Libby was propping her up?

They sat on the expansive back porch of Nora House and watched the pontoons float by in the evening sun.

"I'm so grateful for all you've done, given me, inspired me to do here."

"Wait, wait, nope, you better not be breaking up with me."

"What? No, no that's not it."

"It's just, I settled my divorce, and I'm clear of all those obligations. And I want to buy the cottage from you."

"You don't have to do that! I know I put a lot on your plate when I brought you here. Part of my end of the deal was a free lease on a restaurant and place to stay."

"And it was what I needed, yes, but what I need to make this my life is one hundred percent autonomy."

"I understand, and I respect that. I'm amidst that same push and pull with Aunt Emma, to be honest. So what do you propose?"

"I've got a cash offer for you. Sixty thousand, today, no contingencies for the cottage."

Hope knew the property had the potential to go for three times that. She prayed she wasn't insulting her friend with the offer.

But she also knew that Libby was overwhelmed with things to renovate and the stewardship of Nora House, as Aunt Emma called it.

"You're giving me more than it's worth," Libby said. "It's an eight hundred square foot 1950s cottage that needs a new roof, doesn't have heat, and hasn't been updated since, like, *The Dick Van Dyke Show* was on primetime, first run."

"I'm giving you half of its worth if that. It's charming, and you know it. It's clean and well-built and is right on the water. Taking sixty thousand, you're losing money."

Libby was making the deal sound terrible, the opposite of her normal negotiating strategy.

"No, I mean, that thing was given to me, just like all this stuff Aunt Emma put on my balance sheet. This would be one less thing to renovate, rent, or tear down, are you kidding me? I'm in your debt."

"It is all I need. Actually, it's exactly what I need. Everything here, from the restaurant to finding my Sandbar Sisters, this has changed the trajectory, you know?"

"I know. I hear you like the neighbor too," Libby teased.

"Stop. I'm recently divorced. I need to stay in the shallow end of the dating pool for a bit."

"I understand but are you really sure? I am just carrying the bare minimum on insurance for that place, and I can keep doing that until you're more settled."

"I'm very sure, but I'd be open to half now, half after we get next season at the restaurant under our belts."

"That's kind of nice to hear, that you're planning to be here for another season."

"Yes, I am. We'll close in the fall, and open in May and in between I'm not sure what. Maybe find a heater for the cottage."

"Yeah, you'll need it."

"Libby, no one but Patrick Tate knows this, but I gave Archie everything, our house, our cars, and I signed away alimony."

Libby gave her a look of concern. Hope had figured she'd get that from most people, so she hadn't told anyone.

"He's the one who cheated!" Libby blurted. "You could have had half of the house at least, not to mention support!"

"I know, but I wanted to be done. I kept my winnings, that's my nest egg, and soon I'll insist on a fair rent at the restaurant."

Libby waved her off.

Hope persisted. "I really feel what I'm building there is right. And it's mine. I'm going to buy that part of the building one day, but for now, no more freeloading for lodging."

"You're hardly freeloading. I wanted to make this work for you, make it so you couldn't say no."

"Well, you did. But now, I'm ready to stand on my own two feet. Make my own decisions, right or wrong, without Archie."

"I'm thrilled. Now I just have to figure out what to do about this grant situation."

Libby slid some pictures over to Hope.

"Oh, is this Ellston's on the Pier?"

"It is, it is."

Hope thumbed through them. "The whole block? He's taking the whole block?"

"Yeah, Stirling Stone says his TV show is set to drive interest, make it a little foodie tourist mecca."

"Hmm." Hope looked at the photos. "He bought the block. Well, what do they need the grant for then if Ellston bought it?"

"Wait, what did you say?"

"If Ellston bought the block, what will they use the five hundred thousand for?"

Libby stood up and ran to her kitchen. Hope was slightly concerned her friend would break a hip with how fast she was flinging papers.

She returned to the porch with her laptop.

"That is a very good question, very good. We had to submit detailed plans for our five hundred thousand. It's why I pushed you to come here. I needed that restaurant, among other things."

"Right, yes."

"If Ellston owns the block and he's doing the renovation, or the food channel is or whatever, they'd have to resubmit detailed plans for how they were using the grant."

Libby was now typing on her laptop faster than the human eye could register. The movement of her fingers was slightly terrifying.

J.J. arrived with wine in hand in the midst of Libby's frenzy.

"Whoa, I think Libby just broke the speed barrier with that keyboard. What is she typing?" J.J. raised her eyebrows at Hope and handed her a glass of wine.

"Got me. I think we just let her go. It's like freeform jazz."

"Aha!" Libby said. And then a few minutes later, "NO WAY!"

Finally, Libby looked at her two friends.

"They have resubmitted. Just like the grant rules require. Look, they're doing flowers, benches, a public sculpture. That's what the money is going to go to. They *were* using it like we were —roofs, sidewalks, infrastructure, flowers, and benches."

"Flowers and benches are nice," Hope said.

"Yeah, and guess what, our senior citizens squad did that in Irish Hills—all volunteers. They donated flowers and labor," Libby said.

"Wait, I smell what she's cooking," J.J. said. She went to the files piled on Libby's table. She handed Libby the copies of the million forms they'd submitted.

Libby scanned the fine print and then read it out loud: "The Small Business Downtown Revitalization Authority gives priority to grant applicants in communities that need the funds for vital structure and infrastructure improvements."

"That doesn't sound like flowers and benches and a public art installation."

"No, and while that's lovely, I'm sure our need in Irish Hills is greater than Covert Pier. Thanks to Stirling Stone's medaling," Libby said. And then she started to laugh.

"No offense, but that sounds like evil, super villain laughing," Hope remarked.

"I think it is. Are you okay?" J.J. asked.

"Sorry, yes, I'm okay. I have a call to make. And if I'm right, Stirling Stone just overplayed his hand. He owns a casino. Get it? I have a call to make!"

Libby went in search of her phone.

J.J. sat down where Libby had been. Hope offered her a piece of pizza.

"She's frightening," Hope said.

"Yeah, she is. I'm glad she's on our side."

Hope and J.J. clinked wine glasses. They heard Libby on the phone, presumably talking to the grant committee.

Chapter Twenty-Six

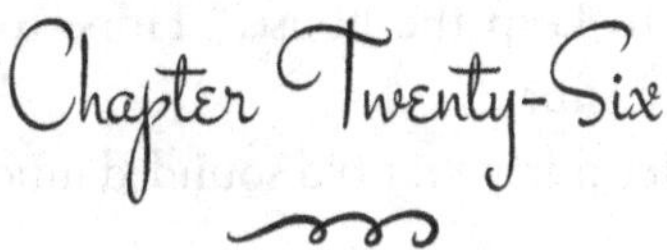

Hope

Hope had done it.

Hope's Table was a success. Well, successful in that it was open, people loved it, and she was learning something new every day.

They'd never filled even close to fifty people, but she had ideas on how to get people to the restaurant. Hope would pay Libby rent next season, if there was the next season, and she'd live in the cottage for now.

Those things felt right, and like she was taking big steps to make the rest of her life the way she wanted it to be.

The last bit of business, as her life shifted from Covington, Kentucky, to Irish Hills, Michigan, was her girls.

Finally, her oldest called her back. She didn't want to fight, but she did wonder about where they were in terms of all the changes that had been visited upon their nuclear family.

"So, I know it was you who snitched on me to your dad."

"He needed to apologize," Julia said. "I thought there was a chance that you'd patch things up."

"Well, he did show up. It was dramatic, to say the least."

"I'm sorry, I just thought, maybe..."

Julia was sweet and had the classic older child proclivity to think it was her responsibility to fix things. To be in charge.

"Dad's going to keep the house," Hope told her, "And the divorce is settled. It's final."

"Oh, okay." Her thirty-year-old sounded much younger at that moment.

She hadn't trashed Archie to the girls. Maybe that was a mistake. They thought of Archie as the victim because she was the one who "ran off." Even though he'd done the cheating, she'd done the leaving.

She didn't tell them about the financial risk Archie had nearly taken with Hope's money.

Should she warn them about Archie's worst qualities, so they weren't caught off guard? Was that protecting them, or was it vindictive?

Hope didn't want to be vindictive. She was a cook. Bitter wasn't a flavor she wanted to serve to the world.

"Do you girls see me as the villain, the one who quit? I hope that's not the case. I will say only this: It was a last straw kind of thing, between your dad and me, beyond the affair."

"I don't see you as the villain, and neither does Sara, well, when I can get a hold of her. But we love Dad too."

"For sure, yes, and I don't want to interfere with that."

"Mom, I've been in relationships, I understand."

Her little girls weren't little girls. She was proud of them and hoped they'd figure out this next phase. The one where they were off being adults, and she was too.

"You know, I may not want your dad here, but I do want you and your sister here. This place is a perfect retreat. If you had a long weekend, you could come to visit, sit by the lake, and check out my restaurant. It's coming together, but I'd love to get your thoughts."

"Thanks, Mom, I appreciate it, but this summer is nuts. I don't think I can get away for a while."

"Sure, well, the door is open, and so is the offer. Should I be worried about Sara? She texts but just hasn't answered any of my calls."

"You know her. She's a free spirit. If she's texting, I wouldn't worry too much about it."

"Okay, well, let's make sure we both keep tabs on her, at least with texts."

"Of course. I love you, and I'm very proud of the restaurant. Honest."

"Thank you, honey. I love you too."

They hung up. It was good to clear the air. Archie was a better man as a father than a husband. That was a deal most mothers would take. But Hope was over being shortchanged by Archie's deficits.

True to her instruction to Julia, she called Sara but didn't expect her to pick up.

"Checking in. Dad and I are officially divorced. I know it's weird to leave this as a voicemail, but you haven't taken my calls in a bit. Love you, are you okay? Getting worried."

Her phone buzzed to indicate a new text was coming in. *Aha!*

"Proud of you, mom. Love u. I'm fine. Call ya later."

Proof of life, that was all you could get some days with adult kids.

* * *

Tuesday, July 12th. Libby had her phone attached to her hand. Every ping, buzz, and alert had her jumping a foot in the air.

They'd decided a day on the sandbar would be the best thing.

The restaurant was closed. J.J. had finished her clients in the morning. And Keith, good-hearted man that he was, had driven them out in the pontoon boat.

They were trying like heck to distract Libby, and the "summer water" that J.J. had in the cooler was helping. But you could see the tension in Libby's brow. You could also see she didn't seem to be eating. Libby was waiting on pins and needles to see if her bid to get the grant committee to reconsider was going to work, since the day she'd realized Covert Pier didn't have the same level of need as Irish Hills.

"You can't let this get to you so much. Have some carbohydrates. You're looking underfed," J.J. said.

Keith put a hand on Libby's shoulder, and she passed on the potato chips that J.J. offered.

Libby remembered a similar setup decades ago when they planned their futures. She had a little feeling of déjà vu. She had been here before. They all had.

"You need to get a degree, just as a backup," Libby had instructed Goldie.

Goldie had waived Libby off and instead took a dip in the water. Turns out Libby had been wrong in that case, though Hope believed Libby had only been wrong a handful of times in her life.

Libby jumped up, and the entire pontoon rocked with the dramatic motion.

"Hey, party foul, my daiquiri didn't make itself," J.J. said.

"Are you having a cardiac event?" Hope asked.

"Look, look!" Libby showed her phone to Hope, who read:

Upon further review, the committee has decided that the Irish Hills application more closely aligns with the mission of the Small Business Downtown Revitalization Authority. Irish Hills is awarded the full amount of the grant, and the funds will be deposited to your organization on the fifteenth of this month and the fifteenth of next month.

"WE GOT IT!" Hope exclaimed to J.J.

"Congratulations, Q!" Keith planted a kiss on Libby, who looked like she might pass out.

"Your phone's ringing," Hope said and handed it back to Libby.

"Well, hello, so you heard." She mouthed "Stirling Stone" to the assemblage of pontoon boat revelers. "Thank you, no, I'm not worried, not in the slightest." She ended the call.

"Well, what was that about?" J.J. asked warily.

"Stone called to threaten me. Well first he congratulated me, then he threatened me."

"That guy is like the split end of billionaires, you trim it off, and it just splits again," J.J. joked.

"Threatened you? What did he say?" Keith had always been their protector, and it was no different now that they were old ladies.

"He said infrastructure won't do a darn bit of good if we don't have customers."

"Well, okay, so he didn't say he'd burn your house down or destroy your family," Hope said.

"No, not that dramatic, except he is right. We have the money, and we have your restaurant, but if we don't start figuring out a way to get people to Downtown Irish Hills, no one's going to eat at that restaurant, or shop at the theoretical shops or rent the hotel we still need to fix up."

"Seriously, get her another drink," J.J. said.

"Actually, the potato chips. I think I need carbs, like you said."

"Well, one problem at a time. You ladies saved the town this week. Next week you'll figure out how to throw a party. No worries," Keith said.

"Keith's right," Hope agreed. "We'll figure it out. One thing at a time, let us celebrate our win. I'm starving."

Hope handed Libby the potato chips, and she ate them like she hadn't eaten in a week. Maybe she hadn't.

For the rest of the day, they stopped strategizing about the future of Irish Hills and just enjoyed the lake.

A day on the lake, with friends, in the summer season, with a little summer water, was all anyone really needed.

Keith turned on the Yacht Rock radio station as they floated the rest of the day away.

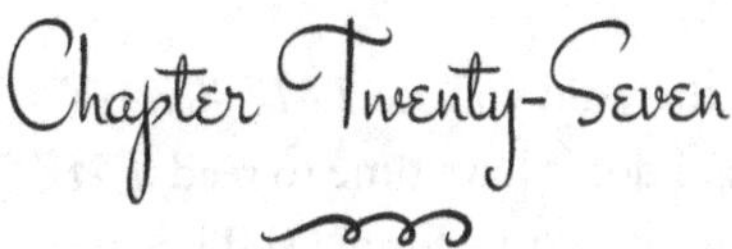

Chapter Twenty-Seven

Libby

Libby was sunburned, but it was a good sunburn, just her shoulders, and just enough to know that even though she was working her butt off, she was also enjoying her life.

Thursday lunch at Hope's Table with Aunt Emma had become her new tradition.

"I like not having too many choices. Have you ever been to Cracker Barrel? It's pages and pages. I don't want to read *War and Peace*. I want an egg sandwich, you know?"

"I do."

Libby had brought Aunt Emma up to speed on the grant.

"Take that, Billionaire Man!"

Aunt Emma and J.J. had taken to calling Stirling Stone 'Billionaire Man' for some reason.

"That's not the end of Stirling Stone," Libby warned. "He's going to do whatever he can to make people avoid Irish Hills."

"It's obviously now a premier, up-and-coming vacation spot. He's vanquished, defeated, sent packing," said Aunt Emma.

"Ha, hardly. I doubt he'll give up. He said as much. But while we use the grant to finish this building, we need to get a gift shop or clothing boutique in this space. But we also need to get good press. Stone went on and on about Chef Ellston and his celebrity clientele."

"Well, about that, did you see *TMZ Today*?"

"Aunt Emma, I don't have time to read *TMZ*."

"Okay, well, look." Aunt Emma slid her state-of-the-art smartphone over to Libby.

Libby didn't have her readers on, but that turned out to be no problem. The text size on Aunt Emma's phone was gigantic.

"Wow, I guess that's one way to solve the readers issue."

"Hmm, just read."

The headline blared; *Goldie Hayes dropped from marquee project!*

"Keep going. She's having a moment, as the kids say."

Oscar nominee's behavior raises eyebrows and insurance premiums.

"This is all just gossip, Aunt Emma."

"Oh, sure, but look at this blind item."

Libby rolled her eyes as her aunt, who'd turned into Rona Barrett all of a sudden, pulled up another story. She read:

A precious metal by any other name's once blinding luster is tarnishing. Sources close to the production of the latest installment of a major movie franchise say the once above-the-title constellation is out in favor of a star with a little less seasoning! Said seasoned twinkler reportedly destroyed her on set trailer, slapped a production assistant, and worse yet, broke the terms of the contract on the way off the lot. Stay tuned to see if the sparkler continues to flame out!

. . .

"Uh, is this English?" Libby asked.

"You just have to read between the lines. Precious metal, obviously your friend Goldie. Tarnish, well, she's used up, getting too old to carry movies, that's the implication. She used to open movies, and now, well, she's not as popular as the younger starlets. It looks like Goldie trashed her dressing room, slapped someone, and is in violation of her contract. They're predicting the worst is yet to come."

"You got all that from this?"

"Yes, it's code."

"What are you saying? I mean, I feel bad for Goldie if it's true, but spell it out."

"Seems to me we have three of five Sandbar Sisters. Why not go get one more?"

"Goldie isn't going to need me to bail her out. She's one of the most famous actresses in Hollywood!"

"Was, not is, didn't you get the point there?"

"I'm not the grim reaper or a buzzard or something."

"No, what you have is a huge hotel that needs renovation. No one else has that kind of cash. Oh, and weren't you saying you needed to compete with that rude celebrity chef man?"

"Yes, yes I was."

"Okay then, go get Goldie."

Libby cocked her head at her aunt, who apparently thought anything was possible.

Could it work? Would Goldie Hayes, formerly Liz Gould, Sandbar Sister charter member, current household name, consider coming back and helping them turn Irish Hills around?

It seemed like a long shot.

But then again, one year ago, she would never have predicted she'd be here, fighting for a town she thought she'd left behind.

She opened her own phone and started searching for flights to L.A.

California might have sunny beaches and movie stars, but Lake Manitou had no sharks and no salt.

Libby would work on her pitch; it was Hollywood, after all.

The Story of the Sandbar Sisters continues in…
Sandbar Summer

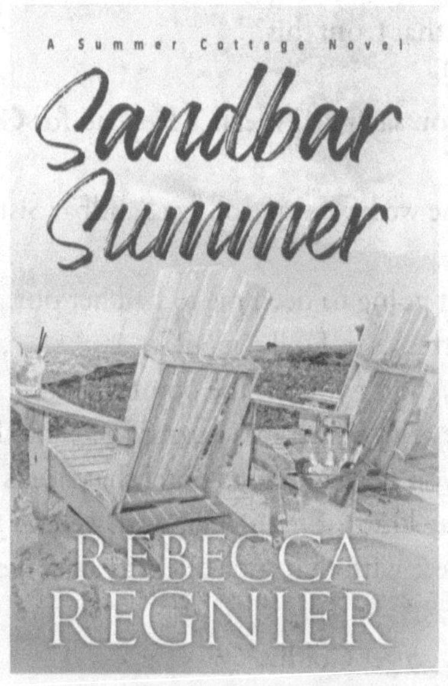

About the Author

Rebecca Regnier is an award-winning newspaper columnist and former television news anchor. She lives in Michigan with her family and handsome dog. Or follow her on one of her socials. She loves share laughs with her readers!

**Sign up for Rebecca's Newsletter
to get a free bonus scene.**
Celebrate Libby Quinn's fiftieth birthday and meet her kids for the first time. Click here for Rebecca's Newsletter and your bonus scene. Visit BeachyReads.com/bonus-scene for more information.

tiktok.com/@rebeccaregnierbooks

facebook.com/rlregnier

instagram.com/rebeccaregnier

bookbub.com/authors/rebecca-regnier